CW00808458

THE KING STREET KIDS

by
Philip Atkinson

* * * * *

The King Street Kids
Copyright © 2012 by Philip Atkinson

Easter—the end begins

When the warm spring wind chased the last of the snow from the fells, the valley smiled with daffodils and coltsfoot, and the returning songbirds put new life into the village of Witton Park. Even without the reminders of ministers and schoolteachers I knew that Easter was special. Naturally special.

Lent, and its lamentably frequent fish dinners, ended with the exquisite boredom of Good Friday; that funless fast-day when religion kept us indoors except to go to Communion at 8.00 a.m., Stations-of-the-Cross at 3.00 p.m., and Benediction at 6.00 p.m. By tradition, our family occupied the third pew from the altar, though my dad always sat behind to facilitate what he called 'necessary disciplinary action' and what we called 'clouts-on-the-lugs.' St. Chad's was a three-room village school that magically transformed into a church when the great partitions folded back like concertinas. The tiny alter at the chapel end, separated from the secular in an alcove with stained glass windows, was accessed from the vestry to the right as you faced it. At St. Chad's, the late service reached its finale when Father McShame hoisted the monstrance high above his head; it was spectacular and mysterious, with incense smoking from the golden thurible whirled by an altar boy with Brylcreemed hair. All this took hours of tortuous kneeling and keeping quiet.

"Good Friday? What's good about it?" asked Jack. A smack from my father focused his attention back on his rosary beads.

We were five in all, my brothers and I, and we sat like Russian dolls along the church bench. Jack was named after my father's brother, a victim of the carnage of Dunkirk. He alone had a middle name - Edward - after my mother's brother who fell from the skies during a bombing mission over Holland in 1941. Jack conformed exactly to the textbook description of a firstborn sibling. He was innovative, decisive, intolerant and fiercely protective. He led us through myriad scrapes and we only saw his qualities of leadership. It never occurred to us that it was he who got us into trouble in the first place. His smile was infectious and he always came through.

Next came Roger, paternal grandfather's namesake. Roger was chalk to Jack's cheese. His dark hair fell in curls over his collar and teachers constantly teased him about it. But he was a cool kid, and although he spoke less often than most boys his age, what he said

3

was always bang on. Bang on, or so esoteric that it made you think he knew what he was talking about. A perfect weapon against dimmer adults.

Ned and Tim were the yin and yang of the gang. Although separated by a year and a bit, they were almost the same size, much to Ned's annoyance. Ned, maternal grandfather's namesake, was dark like Roger, while Tim, named after Mother's favourite cousin, was blond like Jack and me. And while Ned had a nurturing disposition (there was often a frog or mouse in his pockets), Tim was always willing and eager to smash the windows of abandoned houses, bark at cats, or invoke the wrath of grown-ups.

Then, sitting always at the aisle-end of the pew, came me. I was named, as were thousands of boys born that year, on a patriotic whim after the Duke of Edinburgh: Philip. I have not yet forgiven them.

We were born on each other's heels, so to speak, and the phenomenon of so many boys was not unusual in that post war decade. Some say that the glut of males was God's way of making up the numbers wasted in battle. He would seem indeed to work in mysterious ways. And this was the New Britain; victorious and free and, as Prime Minister Harold Macmillan condescendingly put it, we "... had never had it so good..."

Certainly I had never had it so good. The compensation for the masochism of Good Friday was the late afternoon salad, massive and magnificent. Dad's garden allotment behind Park Terrace yielded acres of greens from collards to cress, spring onions to asparagus, sliced cucumbers, fat tomatoes, chicory, chives and chervil. Nestled in the middle of it all on beds of curly cos lettuce were sliced eggs from Ned's chickens plus tinned tuna, tinned salmon, and (sharp intake of breath) tinned shrimp! But special as it was to me, even this memorable meal paled in comparison to the wonderful procession that followed the rigours of rising again.

On Easter Day each year since the beginning of time, the village had held a procession. I know this to be true because Mr. Wicker, a local eccentric, told me so, and he had no reason to lie as far as I could tell. The only person to ridicule the bizarre ranting of 'Nutty' Wicker was Father McShame and, as it seemed to me that it was his job to stifle fun wherever he saw it, I gave great credence to Mr. Wicker. Nutty had rarely set foot in a church, but he owned the

4

bower upon which the statue of the Virgin was carried through the street, and each year he annoyed the priest by adorning it with what the priest called 'pagan plants'—ivy and myrtle—before offering it to the parish for the parade. It was painted green and red and looked very much like one of those pallets Dutchmen carry Edam cheeses on, but Nutty said it was over a thousand years old and, as I said, he had no reason to fib.

"I rather think it would be nice for the parish to have its own bower," Father McShame said each year. "Then we should not have to bother Mr. Wicker every time."

"It is absolutely no bother at all," Nutty countered each year, "It is an honour I look forward to greatly!" Then the two men would look at each other like they knew something we didn't. Which was also true.

"I'd be obliged if you would not refer to the statue as 'the goddess'," was always the parting remark from the priest, and its traditional reply was "Bob's yer uncle!"

On Good Friday morning, on the way home from church, we stopped to watch a man in a suit posting a notice on the gibbet on Black Road. He leaned his sit-up-and-beg bike against the standpipe that had once provided water for horses but had fallen into disuse during the Boer War. Of course, it wasn't a real gibbet, it was the remains of an old hoist that had pulleyed grain sacks into waggons in the pre-industrial days. No one in Witton Park had ever been hanged—except Jakey Jones, the shell-shocked veteran of Flanders Field. But, when he could no longer stand the noise of battle raging inside his head, he hanged himself in his own wash house, so that doesn't count.

For years, certainly all my life, the gibbet was used to post notices. The oldest was made of white enamelled tin and proclaimed in blue lettering, *Bill stickers will be prosecuted*, and of course some wag had scribbled underneath, *Bill Stickers is innocent*. The upright of the hoist was so tall that even when Roger stood on Jack's shoulders he was unable to rob the famous Jackdaw's nest of a year before. It was marvellous to watch the birds labouring to build the nest on the crossbeam. Fortunately, taller kids than us were able to get at the eggs, thus ensuring the crows would not beget offspring with a predisposition for building nests in stupid places.

The man in the suit had a brand-new hammer and four shiny nails. He was very careful not to bash his fingers, and his tongue poked out as he gingerly performed. He was a young man, with sideburns and a ducktail in his hair. When people asked about the notice he shrugged and said he knew nothing and that he was just doing his job. When he'd banged in the last nail, he stepped back from the gibbet and eyeballed the notice for plumb. Then he washed his hands under the standpipe, climbed onto his bike and rode off.

Gyp Williams, a tinker, was the first to read the bulletin. Nothing had been posted there for a very long time, and interest was sharp. Gyp's lips moved when he read and Tim mimicked him behind his back. We sniggered until he turned around and caught us.

"You buggers," he said, clipping Tim's ear, "You'll be laughing on the other side of your faces soon. Category 'D'! Category 'D'!" Then he turned and stormed off toward the Rose and Crown pub. Jack read the notice aloud. It was full of County Hall jargon: herein with; aforementioned; administrative jurisdiction. All I wanted to know was where the other side of my face was so I could laugh on it when the time came.

Category 'D' was the label attached to communities in Britain that had fallen into such states of decay that vermin refused to live there. The government passed a bill in far-off Westminster decreeing that our little village was to suffer what Hitler's bombs had failed to do: it was to be razed. In keeping with Mr. Macmillan's plans for the New Britain, where we had never had it so good, householders would be compensated with a paltry forty-five pounds sterling and the opportunity to rent new houses on new estates in new towns.

"It says we have to shift," my father explained after he'd had a looksee at the notice. "We'll see about that!" Good job he saw it on the way home from the morning service—it was slashed and ripped up when we next passed by on the way home from Stations-of-the-Cross.

"Look what someone did!" I said.

"Yes," said Rodge thoughtfully. "Some people have no respect for property."

On Easter Saturday, amid the confusion of dressing, eating and listening to 'Uncle Mac' on the brown Bakelite wireless, our breakfast was interrupted by a visit from Father McShame. Mother almost turned inside out in her panic. Half-dressed children with jammy faces littered the kitchen. Pyjamas and towels were strewn everywhere and the remains of a late night snack from the evening before sat conspicuously on her draining board among dozens of yesterday's dirty dishes.

"Don't apologize," said the priest. "I was one of sixteen meself!" But he gave us kids a glare that told a different tale and I just knew I'd somehow committed a sin. And when he continued, "I'm sure the boys will be only too willing to lend a hand to clear up." I knew what the trespass was. The last of the toast was wolfed and we began to tidy up. To young boys, of course, all this means is moving stuff from one place to another, and the very best that can be hoped for is that things get no worse. So as soon as Father McShame and Dad went to sit and chat on the front step, Mother shooed us out from under her feet.

The men found they were unable to sit down as the stone steps were still wet from their daily wash. Each morning, rain or shine, the women of the village scrubbed clean the flagstones outside the front doors. Witton Park was built on a slope, and the washing ritual began at the top of each terraced street long before I got out of bed. Our house was second in the row, and as soon as Mrs. Topping was done, she swilled her steps with some rinse water and rapped on our door as the liquid gushed down toward the gutter. Our neighbour's shrill "Patse-e-e!" was a cry that often woke me up.

"You know what this is all about, George?" asked the priest.

"The notice?" my father ventured.

"The bower," said McShame, stone faced. "Wicker's pagan contraption has to be replaced. He's tied corn dollies to it this year. Said something about fertility. Well, we can't have that kind of talk, can we?" I was loitering in the hallway behind them and made a mental note to ask Jack what fertility meant. *("... It's dried fish. You swish it around in water and pour it on the leeks to make 'em bigger.")*

"I suppose not, Father," said my dad.

"Can you make another? I'll get the wood for you and you can start right away. It won't take long, will it? It's just a couple of planks really. I'll take Jack and Roger with me. Good." And back through the house went the priest, gathering my older brothers on the way, and humming Faith of Our Fathers as he disappeared into the

7

tangle of terraced houses. Dad looked wistfully at the Sporting Pink and said, "Ah, well. No horse racing today." Then he ruffled my hair and added, "That's a few shillings the bookie won't get."

Nutty and McShame were both welcomed in our house. The priest was very adept at collecting remarkably good cast-offs from the richer members of his flock. Once the cast-offs had price tags in them and it became apparent that they hadn't belonged to anyone else after all. My mother was embarrassed to learn this, and my father must have felt a bit inadequate, but I was glad. For the life of me I couldn't figure out who the rich people of our village were; except for a suspicion that it might be the Wymans, who kept fruit on their sideboard even when nobody was sick.

Wicker turned up now and again with one of two things; either he had something from the fields and hedgerows or his garden allotment that we could eat, or else he had an enormously complicated shaggy-dog story to share. But on that Saturday, as I sat on the upturned rain barrel in our back yard watching my dad work, I saw Nutty's happy gnarled face rise slowly above the gate and smile upon the bower project that was just under way. Dad looked at him sheepishly and began to say something, but Wicker seemed to know what was going on and didn't mind a bit.

"I know how the old one's put together, George. I'll help if you like," he said. My father was such a trusting man that he accepted the help gladly. It never dawned on him that Nutty's assistance might irk the parish priest. As if by magic, Wicker produced several lengths of hand-hewn wood from behind his back. They were of suspiciously similar dimensions to the pieces of timber Jack and Rodge had brought from the presbytery, but had a much earthier, warm look about them, and I could see flecks of red and green paint here and there.

"I've already got the wood," my dad said, "I've just got to saw it to length and drill it." Nutty raised his eyebrows, smiled at me, and said,

"Beware the oak, it draws the stroke; Avoid the ash, it courts the flash; Look to hawthorn, it'll keep you from harm!"

"Actually, it's pine," said Dad.

"Oh, gosh. No good at all," replied Nutty. "It'll smell like toilet cleaner." That worked. My dad's nostrils flared and his lip curled at

8

the thought. So they took the sanded down pieces of wood, which even I could see were just the old bower disassembled and sanded, and soon the two were a-hammering and whistling away, chattering and joking and teasing me with questions I could not answer. They thought it immensely funny to ask me what the length of a piece of string was. I can still see them laughing, in my mind's eye. I still don't get it. Two hours and four cups of tea later, the bower was complete; dowelled, glued and painted. Excepting the glossiness of the new paint, it looked exactly like the old one.

The Easter procession was a wonderful ceremony, we didn't even have to sit through the Mass in Latin. It attracted all the villagers regardless of their beliefs, and even folk from the isolated hamlets that were scattered throughout the dale. Two little boys in bright white shirts and blue sashes paced carefully behind the Easter Queen, ensuring her train stayed well above the ground. This year's chosen one was Margret Molloy, whose family called her Peggy and was known at school as Jam-and-bread. She was decked out as a bride in miniature, and a garland of forget-me-nots and baby's breath held her hair back from her face. Most everyone went 'ahh...' when she passed.

Bring flowers of the rarest, bring blossoms the fairest ... piped the clear, fresh choir of children ... *From garden and woodland and hillside and dale* ... I warbled along with the rest, drunk on the heady floral perfume that filled the chapel ... *Our glad hearts are swelling, our voices are telling, the praise of the loveliest flower of the May* ... and all the time Nutty smiled and nodded.

The parishioners fell in behind the two boys and the procession went out of the chapel, round the schoolyard, out of the Boy's gate, twenty yards down Baltic Terrace, back in through the Girl's gate and into the chapel. Painfully short, I always thought. But in years past there had been problems with Protestant hecklers. It was swell to know from Father McShame that *they* weren't going to heaven. When it was over and everyone was well and truly blessed, dismissed and on their way home, the priest motioned to my dad.

"George, about the bower," he said quietly, "It looks great. I'm sure Mr. Wicker will never know the difference." I could see the pain in my father's face as he struggled with the dilemma of whether or not to come clean.

"And the shelf you made for the church porch with the extra wood is very nice. Lovely piney smell."

Homespun Fun

Everyone seemed to be somewhere else so I amused myself by throwing little bits of gravel at the gas lamp outside our house at the top of King Street. The object of my game was to get one of the stones through the loop formed by the iron support arms just beneath the glass lantern. The very first stone I threw smashed the glass. I couldn't believe it, but there it was—the tinkling of the shards and a hurried exit as my cowardly legs took off in the direction of anywhere that wasn't King Street. I heard a door open as old Mrs. Brunton, our neighbour across the street, put out the cat. I prayed I'd made it around the corner before she saw me; down Albion Street and right at the bottom. It suddenly seemed like the perfect time to visit Woodside, a hamlet some half-mile away.

I was leaning against the bright red of the telephone box at the east end of the village, trying to catch my breath, when an arm shot out of nowhere and grabbed hold of my Sloppy-Joe tee-shirt. I expected the worst and was instantly on the defensive.

"I couldn't help it," I cried, closing my eyes in anticipation of the smack that would surely warm my ears. "It was an accident, honest!" Honesty was not within a hundred miles.

"What's up with him?" asked a surprised voice. It was Monty McBain, his watery features contorted as though confronted with something from space. With him, serving as guardian of a handful of my clothing, was Danny Bligh. Danny was part of an unchanging equation that said Danny Bligh equals trouble, and went on Danny Bligh plus more boys equals more trouble. I had an idea that he'd be up to no good and as always would be on the look out to recruit partners in crime. Monty McBain (almost always referred to by his full name) was of little value here, being rather poorly off in the departments of physical stature and grey matter, tragically so in the latter respect.

"What fettle, kid?" asked Danny, smiling one of his beguiling smiles. That smile pulled him out of more trouble than enough, and conversely led me into more than I care to remember. We were best mates at school; sat together, played together and won together. We never lost at anything. He was one of those kids who would change the rules if the game didn't go his way, and he always got away with it because he was everybody's best friend. Besides which he'd bash you if you didn't agree. He had butter-blond hair. Women would stop him in the street and run their fingers through it or ruffle it up, which annoyed him greatly. It wasn't until years later that it occurred to me that the hair was the reason we were so easily spotted performing our mischievous escapades. What did he have in mind to fill this particular day?

"Blocky," said Danny.

Blocky! I could hardly believe it, for the game was merely a variation on hide-and-seek and could not likely get us into any trouble. I was delighted.

"Of course I'll play," I said, "I was going to Woodside but I don't mind a bit of Blocky." Danny smiled and elected me on block; that is, they got to hide, I got to seek. The block was a steel drainpipe, one of which adorned the gable end of every terrace. Black and ugly, they represented state-of-the-art British plumbing. This one, unlike most, was in good repair, although sod proliferated in the gutters and rain flowed where it would. During downpours the red brick walls looked for all the world as if they wept, and the mean miner's houses seemed to huddle closer together for consolation and warmth. In order to score a block, Danny decided that it would be O.K if the hiders just hit the drain-pipe with a stone, thus eliminating the slightest chance of my beating him there should it come down to a last minute sprint. As seeker, I was not allowed that concession and actually had to touch the pipe with my hand. Three times.

"What if we bust the drain pipe?" I asked.

"Doesn't matter," said Danny. "They'll pull everything down anyway. My dad says we're moving to the new estate at Woodhouse Close or mebbe Newton Aycliffe. Everyone is."

"We're not," I said. "My dad says we'll stay here."

"Nobody's allowed," Danny was confident, and it came across as a threat almost. "The Council's sent a notice." And there it was again. The notice. Yet my dad had been confident that we weren't going to leave Witton Park, and nothing Danny said could convince me otherwise.

11

"Why does he want to stay here?" Danny asked. "It's going to be great at Aycliffe. They've got building sites and a beck and an old rifle range and everything." I still wasn't convinced.

"But there's tons of great places to play here. The river, the gill fields, and..." I played my ace card. "The guts."

The guts was, …well…exactly that. Each week the local butcher's shop had a couple of cows delivered. They went in alive and kicking and came out as Sunday roasts, steaks and mince. What was left was carted to a remote location near the river and dumped. Guts. Heads, tails, stomachs, innards and eyeballs. All in glorious colour.

We had been forbidden to visit the guts under the threat of physical retribution.

"I'll tan you silly if you go near that place," Dad had said with an unintended but appropriate pun. But the place held such a morbid fascination that I had ignored the threat several times, and always with Danny Bligh.

"Well…" I could tell by his tone that I had at least presented a dilemma. "Everybody's leaving. You won't have anyone to go to the guts with." That had not occurred to me. I looked up at water seeping over the top of the drainpipe and wondered why no one had bothered to clean it out.

"One, two, three..." I began to count, eyes to the pole. Monty McBain took off hotfoot in pursuit of his idol and mentor.

"Bugger off!" I heard Danny instruct his heel-trotting protégé, and with the obedient and unemotional reply, "Right ho!" the little chap toddled off on a tangent to somewhere else.

"... ninety-nine, a hundred! If you're not off, you're blocked," I said with extreme conviction, then added just in case, "By one, two, three!" I turned about and was caught between mirth and contempt. Within spitting distance there was a lamp similar to one I had destroyed earlier. It was the most obvious hiding place around and no self-respecting kid over five years old would contemplate its use but, almost predictably, there were the scuffed toes of Monty McBain's gym shoes poking out from the bottom. He peeked out. I saw him. He knew I'd seen him; I knew he knew. Yet his head disappeared and the toes remained motionless. When I looked around the lamp-post I saw he had his eyes tight shut and his forefingers firmly plugged into his ears.

"Come on, you're blocked," I told him. He didn't stir. I think he was holding his breath too, as there were definite signs of his skin undergoing a colour change. I flicked the end of his nose hard. As I was about to do it again a large pearl-shaped teardrop formed in the corner of his eye.

"I'm sorry," I began, but no sooner had I lowered my defences than he nipped smartly past me and legged it toward the block. In a split second I recovered my senses and my hand shot out and grabbed the seat of his pants. Khaki shorts have a fair amount of give in them and he managed to advance one or two steps further before he realised he was in fact stationary, despite his legs still churning away. With a mighty haul I pulled him backwards until he sat in the dust, confronted with the spectacle of my good self blocking him at the pipe. I felt quite good about such a quick capture, even if Blind Pew could have found the little clot just as easily.

As tradition required, Monty McBain was incorporated into the service of the seeker and the two of us set out in search of Danny, of whom, however, there was no sign after three sweeps of the area. We searched again and after ten minutes (days in hide-and-seek chronology) we gave up and called his name, assuring him that he was the outright winner if only he would show himself. When he did just that, we were totally unprepared for his re-entry to the land of the tangible. Danny had been hiding inside an outhouse.

In those dark days our village was one of the last places left in Britain to have outside lavatories. At the back of each yard stood what was known locally as 'the netty.' It backed onto the little muddy lane that ran between the rows of terraced houses and was, in fact, an earth midden. All refuse, both household and human, was deposited into the netty through a hole in the wooden seat. The enclosed space below was quite large; almost big enough for a small boy to stand up in. Each Thursday, they were emptied via a short door that opened into the lane and dusted with pink germicide by stalwarts from Bishop Auckland Rural District Council — the 'midden men.'

Replacing the outhouse with an indoor toilet had been job one for my dad back in 1945. The way he told it, my mother had him replace what she called 'the abomination' almost the day they had moved in. It was one of his best arguments for not moving to Aycliffe, where, rumour had it, every single house had indoor toilets.

13

As we walked back toward the pole to begin a new game of blocky, we suddenly became aware of someone singing in an ethereal, thin voice. It was Billy Beaker, the snivelliest kid that ever was—betrayer of plans and friend of authority. Time and again Beaker had told tales on his classmates to gain favour with our teacher, Mrs. Trout. She in turn dispensed the kind of punitive measures we would rather have done without: caning, lines and, worst of all, she sometimes hauled us in from the football field to partner girls in dancing class.

"It's Beak-nose-Beaker!" said Monty McBain. Danny hated Beaker through and through and whenever the opportunity arose, he punished him for his blatant disloyalty to his schoolmates. As we neared the source of this wailing rendition of *Hound Dog*, we realised with great delight that the hollow and ghostly sound could only be coming from the netty at the back of Beaker's yard.

Danny raised a finger to let us know he wanted silence. We hushed, our faces contorted with the effort of trying to stifle the laughter. This was a heaven-sent opportunity as only two days before we had had to suffer at school while Beaker poured out his heart to Mrs. Trout concerning his mortal fear of being bitten by a rodent while using the toilet. Before he sat down on the throne, he said, he would shine a flashlight and thrash around with a pea-cane to be certain he was alone in there.

Carefully, silently, we slipped the latch on the trap door; it sprang ajar. The singing grew louder. Stealthily we opened the door wide, and there before us hung Beaker's lily-white bum, oblivious to the danger that lurked below. The song changed with divine inspiration to *Poison Ivy*, and Monty McBain had the one and only brainstorm of his life. He disappeared around the corner of the house opposite, then returned brandishing a two-foot long nettle in his hand. It was perfect.

Gently, Danny took hold of the naked stem and inserted the plant into the darkness before us. I made a few scratching noises to stimulate Beaker's rat theory, then Danny Bligh mercilessly trailed the venomous wand across the bare cheeks above him. Priceless must have been the sight of the stung songster's face. Alas we could not see it! But we did see hear him trip over the shorts around his ankles in the ensuing scream-filled flight to the house. Happy days!

When I eventually got home I found that Mrs. Brunton had seen me trash the lamp after all, and my mother laid me across her knee. It was a strange walloping, as I laughed all the way through. Just as the first stroke made contact, she said. "This'll sting your backside!"

Washday Blues

Monday was the day my mother washed clothes. In fact, it was the day almost every mother in Witton Park washed clothes. As soon as the kids were packed off to school, the toil began. In our back kitchen there was a washing machine of sorts. Actually, it was just a cream-coloured boiler with a mangle attached, but when the water reached piping-hot, Mother would add soap powder and plunge the laundry under the surface with her wash stick. Then she would pummel the clothes—lifting and twisting and turning for as long as it took to shift the dirt. Colloquially, this was known as possing, and it was done with a poss stick.

Poss sticks looked to me like milking stools nailed to the bottom of a spade handle. Just like many of the women in the village and all over the North, my mother had once owned an authentic poss tub. Traditionally, these tubs were made by sawing through a beer barrel at the third hoop and upending it. When my dad brought home the gas boiler she was as proud as a peacock and the envy of the neighbours.

I had spent Sunday night dreaming about Newton Aycliffe and trying to think of how well the boiler would sit with all the other modern miracles I had heard existed in that far-off Utopia. In the tortuous otherworld of dreamland, the machine had taken over the house and I had to save everyone from its foaming wrath. Consequently, I had not slept well and woke up hot and sticky and in the mood for nothing more than a day off school.

"Come on, Philip," Mam urged. "You'll be late." Jack and Rodge had been up and gone since seven as they were alter boys and had to be at the chapel for the morning service. The clock was ticking its way toward nine and Ned and Tim were already in their navy-blue gabardine coats and shoving as much toast inside them as they possibly could.

"I'm not well," I said to Mam as she returned from hanging out a line full of washing. "I'm proper poorly." I didn't really expect to get much sympathy and I was bang on as far as my brothers were concerned.

"Nice try," said Ned.

"Please Mammy," mimicked Tim, "I'm poorly." He did it really well and I thought if I sounded that pathetic I might as well give it up and go to school. Mam stepped up to me and looked long and hard into my face. She gently pulled down my left eyelid and sighed heavily.

"You do look a bit pale," she said. "All right, you stay home today." I wish I had a photograph of my brothers' faces from that moment. The vocal protests diminished with the distance they travelled from the door and by the time they had gone completely, I was sitting in the horsehair couch at the side of the living room.

"You sit there and be good," said Mam. "I've got such a load of work to get through I won't be able to run after you all day." I snuggled down in the chair and by golly I began to feel better right then and there. It's wondrous how a day off can cheer one up.

Mother began the tedious business of gathering and sorting laundry. In Beaker's house they had something called a hamper. Beaker actually put his dirty clothes in it and his mother didn't have to walk two miles around the house picking the stuff up as my mother did. But it seemed to me that if you added together all the miles my brothers and I would have to walk to a hamper every time we took off a tee-shirt or something, it would far exceed the distance Mam had to walk. So all in all, we were doing the right thing by simply dropping clothes where they came off. Almost as soon as I had snuggled in, a shrill voice came in from the street.

"Patseeee... the coalman's here!" It was the signal for Mam to step outside and raise the clothes prop.

"Oh, no, it can't be," she said, "I've only just hung stuff out!"

The coalman was Mr. Gilmour. He owned the two-ton flatback lorry that brought sacks of coal each week around the village. He always drove down the street and dropped the huge filthy bags at customer's front doors, despite the fact that everyone's coal cellar was at the back. When the women demanded that he make delivery at the back door, he said he couldn't get the lorry down the narrow back lanes. Everyone knew that wasn't true as the midden men emptied the outhouses in the back lanes every Thursday and their truck was even bigger than Gilmour's. In order to get the lorry down the street, the washing lines had to be lifted so the newly cleaned clothes didn't brush against the dirty coal sacks. As the coalman progressed down the street, each woman would come out and heft the long clothes prop high to let him pass.

"Why do you always have to come on a washday?" was the other question he was asked often.

"I have to start somewhere," he replied. "And Witton Park's farthest from the pit." The logic made no sense to me and I had heard women say he did it just to pay them back. About a year previously, a young man had appeared on the scene selling coal at a lower price than Gilmour. He had been good-looking, witty and never delivered on a washday. Every last customer in the village had bought coal from him and Gilmour had lost both money and face. Unfortunately, the young coal merchant wasn't the best businessman in the world and he had gone under when the taxman came to collect at year's end. There was no choice but to revert to Gilmour and that's when he started to deliver on Mondays.

When the call came for my mother to raise the washing line she was up to her elbows in soapsuds and had washed the last towel. Frantically she looked around for something to dry her hands on. She grabbed a yellow pullover from the mountain of kid's clothes in the middle of the floor and rubbed her arms.

"Come on, missus," called Gilmour. "I haven't got all day!" Mam rubbed even faster and hurried out through the front door.

"Sorry, Mr. Gilmour," she said. "You're not usually here until late in the morning. I'll have to take in the sheets altogether." Normally the coalman came much later when the sheets were dry and lines were filled with shorter stuff like tea towels and nappies. It was a sort of unwritten code that everyone played by.

"I suppose you'll be moving to Aycliffe, will you?" he asked.

I beat my mother to it and piped up, "Over my Dad's dead body."

"I thought you were sick..." I dived for cover behind the front door. I was surprised to hear Mam tell Mr. Gilmour that it was likely we would move along with everyone else. I had thought we were all sticking together in this and standing behind Dad. But, as I was wrong about most things concerning grown-ups, I wasn't as surprised as I might have been.

"It's all bloody smokeless," said the coalman. "I hope you're all happy sitting around false fireplaces and bone-dry central heating."

I couldn't imagine a house without a fireplace. Where would we put Dad's armchair? Mam didn't seem particularly phased.

"There's fireplaces," she said. "But they burn coke not coal. Much cleaner, much warmer..."

"Much more expensive!" he interrupted. "I just hope you'll all be so very happy!"

"So that's why you're early is it? Can't sell coal in Aycliffe so we have to suffer for it? Well," she raised herself to her full height of five-foot nothing, "Bad cess to you!" And she skimmed along the clothesline and took down all the wet washing and brought her wicker basket back indoors.

I didn't like Mr. Gilmour. He had once offered me a lollipop and as I reached out in glee he snatched it away and put it in his own mouth. "Have to be quicker than that!" he laughed. He climbed back into the coal lorry and slowly drove it another ten houses along. I closed the front door and went back to the kitchen where my mother was possing away furiously at the next batch of dirty laundry.

She liked to sing when she worked, although she had so little regard for her own voice that it was always hard to make out any words and if she thought you were listening she would simply hum the tune. I suddenly felt sad watching her at the sink. A wedge of bright sunlight came through the glass and put bronze highlights in her black hair. She had been working non-stop since before we were out of bed and the dint in the pile of laundry seemed awfully small. I just knew she'd be washing for two more days to get it under control. During which time of course my brothers and I would be doing our best to climb trees, fall down, roll in mud and get into all manner of clothes dirtying situations.

"Can I help?" I said.

Mam stopped dead in her tracks. Slowly she turned and looked over her shoulder at me. "Bless me!" she said. "I'd almost forgotten you were there, Philip." Again she took up the yellow pullover and dried her hands. "Shall we have a cup of tea?"

"I'll get the teapot," I offered. I stepped up on a chair to reach the cupboard where the brown-betty was kept and was immediately aware from my mother's groan that I'd done something wrong. When I looked down I saw I had stepped onto a neat pile of towels she had just wrung out.

"Oops..."

"Come down," she said. "I'll get it. And let's have another look at you first." She took me around the waist and lifted me back to the floor then looked again under my eyelid. I prayed she would still find whatever she'd found first thing that morning, but oh no... she was beaming.

"You look much better! Maybe you'll be able to go to school this afternoon." Suddenly I felt even worse than I had when I woke up.

"But Mam..."

"We'll see after you've had a cuppa," she said in that way she had of cutting off further protest. "Go out and play for ten minutes while I brew up." I was doomed and as I walked out into the late spring sunshine, I decided never to offer to help ever again.

Just down the street, Mr. Gilmour had parked his coal lorry over to the side and was talking to old Mrs. Jefferson who always invited him in for his mid-morning cup of tea and digestive biscuit so he would knock a bit off her bill. The wheels on the right-hand side of the lorry were sunk deep in the gutter and it tilted over at a precarious angle. It was an ex-army vehicle, still painted khaki-green under the layers of black coal dust. The wheels were much higher off the ground than the top of my head and the rubber tyres were wondrous to behold. Thick tread still remained on the outsides although the middles were completely bald. In those days before roadworthiness checks, bald tyres were more the norm than the exception. I was admiring the great wheels when I looked down into the gutter and saw a newly-spent matchstick. Now, I couldn't believe this had appeared for any other reason than that I was supposed to make use of it. And the most sensible thing a boy can do with a matchstick in one hand and a lorry at the other, of course, is to poke said matchstick into the air valve and deflate the tyre.

As the air hissed from the tyre I felt a sudden guilt. I was suddenly aware of the clothing I had stepped on not ten minutes earlier and I realised that letting the tyre down might not be the smartest thing I'd ever done. I pulled out the matchstick and threw it back into the gutter. But the hissing continued. Upon closer inspection I found that a bit of the matchstick had broken off and was jammed firmly against the pin in the valve so that the air kept coming out. I did what I always did in such situations—checked to see if anyone was looking then ran away. I scooted down King Street, turned right and returned to the house via the back lane, along which I was certain Mr. Gilmour would not venture.

"Here you are, Son," said Mam, sliding a pot of tea across the red gingham oilcloth on the table. "How are you feeling?"

"Oh, I think I might be able to go to school now." Well, of course that caused concerned wrinkles on my mother's brow. She looked again under my eyelid and asked me to put my tongue out.

"Hmm... I suppose..." she murmured. I thought for sure she could tell what I'd been up to and I wondered at the same time how the tyre was doing. I didn't have long to wait to find out. A wailing cry of anguish sounded from the street five minutes later, and Mr. Gilmour was cursing like a trooper. Mam and I ran to the door and looked out. Every other neighbour was doing exactly the same thing. Like a broken old man, the lorry had lurched over so far that several bags of coal had spilled off onto the street and Mrs. Jefferson had a small shiny black mountain at her doorstep. It looked to me that the lorry might even fall on its side, but the coal merchant quickly climbed into the driver's seat and drove to flatter ground, taking Mrs. Jefferson's laundry along for the ride. When he got out again, I could tell he was suspicious and it was just a matter of time before he put two and two together and came up with me.

I need not have worried, though. Old Mrs. Jefferson came bounding out of her house with a spring in her step that hadn't been seen in years, brandishing a black umbrella with a raven-head handle.

"Me bloody washin'," she cried. "Look at me bloody washin'!" and she set about Mr. Gilmour with gusto. The neighbours were delighted to encourage her, shouting and whooping as he beat a hasty retreat to the safety of his cab.

"You can whistle for your money," said Mrs. Jefferson. "Wait till my son Eric hears about this! He'll knock yer block off!" At this point my mother turned to me. I must have been beet-red and I stretched a sheepish grin across my face.

"Are you responsible for this?" she said coldly. But I had the perfect counter.

"Are we really moving to Newton Aycliffe, Mam?" Her face fell as she realised I'd overheard her conversation with Gilmour.

"Get inside and give your face a lick," she said. "You'll be in plenty of time for the afternoon classes if you set off now." I needed no second hint. This had been a close one and as I climbed the hill to Black Road I turned back to survey the scene. The coal lorry had chugged away on three good wheels and the women in King Street, including my mother, were helping Mrs. Jefferson to scoop the unexpected windfall of free coal back into sacks and through to the cellar around the back. Peace settled again on the village and down the street row after row of white sheets flapped in the blustery breeze.

The Picturehouse

Friday was a favourite day for everyone in the village. Father McShame always told us that the Sabbath was more important, yet it was never greeted with as much enthusiasm as the week's last workday. For us it had three main events: school finished for the weekend, cinema night, and the weekly communal bath. The bath was something I looked forward to immensely, but I know other kids dreaded it. Perhaps they didn't receive the same care and attention my ever-patient mother and my ever-gentle father gave.

We bathed every day, of course, but during the week it was in the scullery and not the enamelled splendour of the bathtub as it was on Fridays. The tub stood on eagle-claw feet and was spacious enough to hold three kids with room to spare. At the sloping end, the enamel was chipped in a shape like the map of Spain. There were no taps, and all water had to be carried from the scullery. Above the great ceramic sink in the back kitchen was a teeny-weeny water heater that my father called a geyser. It measured out about a pint of hot water (if you were lucky) before the thermostat clicked and it went cold again. Winters were never much fun first thing in the morning! Encouraged by clichés like, 'It'll make a man of you' and 'Don't be soft,' we plunged our hands into the icy water and splashed it all over ourselves. This was followed by a bout of shivering and shaking and a somewhat sadistic rubdown with coarse towels. How those towels scratched! The trick was to get one after it had been used so that it was somewhat softer than a newly laundered one.

"This wouldn't happen if we had a proper bathroom like those lovely new houses in Aycliffe," Mam said quietly.

"You needn't set your heart on moving there," replied Dad with stern resilience. "I spent good money fitting this place out with an inside toilet and a perfectly adequate heater." Still we shivered.

On that Friday the bathtub was filled with pail after pail of hot water carefully transported by the old man from stove to bath. He loved it and sang and whistled (though not at the same time) all the while. A special treat was to have him wash your hair for you. It never hurt; he was rough and thorough as only a father knows how. Before the penultimate gallon went into the tub, a handful of Lux soap flakes was added and the first bathers had the great pleasure of flailing the surface to whip up mountains of snow-white suds.

At six o'clock, ready for inspection, there was a line-up of angelic little boys awaiting their pocket money: tallest on the right, shortest on the left, hair plastered down to our heads, shiny, beaming faces belying what would happen in the following few hours at the Kozy Kinema. I never heard this name until years after it had been demolished. We didn't even call it a cinema. To us it was 'the picturehouse,' or sometimes—because kids had a 50/50 chance of coming home with head-lice—the 'Loppy Opera.' In the background, Dad's Bakelite wireless squeaked out the latest hit from Billy Fury and we were all in the Friday mood as the coins were meted out. Jack and Rodge got one-and-threepence each and Ned, Tim and myself were each given a shilling. Nobody complained about the seeming inequity; they were older, right? Only fair they got more. We knew exactly what to spend it on, too. The pictures cost, on Friday night, first house, eightpence. That left the big lads with sevenpence and the little 'uns with fourpence. This was spent across the road at Quadrini's, the Italian ice-cream parlour. Nobody bought ice cream, of course, not for the pictures. The statutory requirement was a faceful of Anglo bubble-gum. One such resinous confection all but filled the mouth, so my brothers bought three, at a penny each. They mulched these simultaneously, and, I might add, with great difficulty, throughout the 'B' picture until they were pliable enough to facilitate blowing; whence great pink bubbles would swell periodically from their lips. I purchased only one of these things, preferring to spend the other threepenny bit—to my brothers' embarrassment—on a Lucky Bag (*only babies get Lucky Bags*). Ned and Tim spent their last penny on either a Spanish liquorice-stick or a 'Penny Arrow' toffee bar.

Jack and Rodge spent their remaining coins on 'Jubblies.' These were triangular shaped orange-flavoured ices that required mammoth suck-muscles to extract their juice after the initial dozen licks. Often you'd see someone slurping one of these things with pop-alley eyes and a feint blue tinge about the face. As I recall they didn't taste all that good but as flavour was a secondary element in their purpose it didn't matter much.

The lights dimmed; they were still the old gas mantles and I loved to watch them magically shrink down while their hiss was hushed and the cinema was plunged into darkness. The tomfoolery began almost at once; pinching and pulling as the film began. Cries of delight filled the theatre as John Wayne entered to the strains of '*She wore a yellow ribbon*'. It was always John Wayne. Unless it was Elvis Presley. We cheered the goodies and we hissed the baddies and we made kind of puking sounds when the actors kissed. Occasionally someone would fart—always good for a giggle, especially if the soldiers were hiding from the Injuns and were trying to be particularly quiet. The film snapped during the performance and we stamped like hell in unison. Clouds of dust flew up from the wooden floor and we all sang 'Why are we waiting?'

During the break, the lights went up and Jack and Rodge scanned the sea of heads in hopes of finding one covered in red hair. Now there were only two kids in our age group who possessed this phenomenon. One of them was Lenny Capper—a bit of a woosie who only went to the pictures on a Saturday with his mam and dad. The other was a certain Billy Beaker who, as luck would have it, sat in the third row, centre aisle, some ten or twelve rows in front of us. Beaker was a doubly good find as he not only had the dreaded 'ginger nut,' but was possessed of those other prize targets, sticky-out ears.

"There's bugger-lugs Beaker!" hissed Rodge. A delighted smile showed on all five faces. Now, I don't know why it is that kids with red hair get picked on so much, but it is unquestionably a fact that they do. I suppose it's because they're a bit different and so it's expected almost. Like getting into a fight and knowing you'll win 'cos the other kid's called Cyril. Fact of life. Anyway, the lights went down again and the picture resumed. Six rows ahead of us loomed the unmistakable outline of tonight's victim. Against the brilliance of the screen was silhouetted the flat black image of Beaker's head looking for all the world like a taxi with its doors open.

"Silent routine," whispered Jack. The film a week earlier had been '*The Cruel Sea*' starring Jack Hawkins. We all quietened down. "Load tubes one and two," he went on. Rodge sucked the last from the compacted remains of the 'Jubblie' and seeing Jack at the same stage said,

"Tubes one and two loaded, sir," Ned began to make a doink, doink sound that sounded remarkably like ASDIC and we giggled so much we almost gave the game away. "Starboard two points, Mr. Bosun." Nobody knew what that meant but Rodge replied,

"Starboard two points, aye-aye." Our very lives seemed to be in the balance and my heart skipped a beat as Jack gave the dreadful order.

"Destroyer sighted...bearing three, three, zero...fire both tubes!" Quick flicks of the wrist sent the iceballs flying through the blackness towards the unsuspecting target. Torpedo number one found its mark with a precision with which the Royal Navy would have been ecstatic. It caught Beaker right at the joint of ear and skull, and burst in the cinemascopic light with a spray of incandescence. The initial 'hit' caused the target to retreat somewhat rapidly into the turtleneck pullover in which it was encased, with the result that the second missile missed completely—only to make contact with the curious visage of the kid in front who had chosen that exact moment to look around. Oh, never look back! It smashed him right in the mouth. Though there was no serious damage the sheer terror in his eyes was a delight to behold! This was better than we'd have dared hope.

Unfortunately the fifty or so kids round about laughed too and it attracted the attention of the 'usherette.' I have used that word in as loose a sense as the language will allow, for in this case the usherette was an unshaven old scrag-bag in his seventies. He was baldy. And he always had this fag hanging from his mouth that always had two inches of dottle on it. I marvelled that it never fell off.

"Right," he scowled, "Take a walk!" We protested, naturally, but in those days it was widely accepted that any adult had the right to 'clag-yer-lugs' and he did this with great effect. So reluctantly we left; much to the delight of one little pleb in the back row. He pushed his wire-rimmed specs further up on his nose and stretched his thin lips into an even thinner smile.

"Heh, heh!" he went as we passed.

"Heh, heh!" said Jack, plunging his wad of gum into the kid's hair.

The Soap Box

My father had been reading, for the hundredth time, the letter from county hall telling him his house had been placed under a compulsory purchase order and that our family would be reaccomodated in rented housing in our choice of Woodhouse Close or Newton Aycliffe. He hadn't liked getting it, and I could tell he still didn't like having it.

"Our choice? Our choice? I was on cross-Atlantic convoys," he said. "Malta. Singapore. I don't see why I have to be robbed by these pen-pushers at county hall." I couldn't see the correlation between ploughing the ocean waves and having your house demolished but I'm sure there was one. I could see that he was deeply concerned and of course I took advantage of his distraction to ask for money.

"Here's a tanner," he said absently. I accepted a shiny silver sixpence with silent delight. Dad never got angry except in very short bursts, at which time he might shout or smack the ear of a passing son. Otherwise, the energy of his wrath was spent in its own eruption and he always saw reason if it was there to be seen. This time, however, he seemed bent on doing something about the situation.

"I'm going to do something about this situation," he said. "I'll get up on my soap box and talk to everyone. We're not going to take this." And he folded the letter back into its envelope and left the room.

As I sat before the flames of the coal fire, rolling the tanner from hand to hand, I wondered about his time in the navy. It was always difficult to get him to talk about the war. I was certain that he'd played an important role, of course, as he had almost as many medals as Audie Murphy, the American war hero. My grandfather told me that Americans ate cornflakes for breakfast and that at the bottom of every box was a medal. And that each year on his birthday, President Eisenhower showered medals from the upper windows of the White House and that if you could catch one you could wear it.

Then and there, as I watched my determined father stride off to fight the injustice of bureaucracy as he had previously gone to curb the spread of Hitler's fascism, I decided to build a life-size facsimile of H.M.S. Nelson—my dad's ship. And then I thought about how far we lived from the sea and how much wood it would require and how I didn't know the first thing about shipbuilding. So I took the next logical step and decided to build a go-cart instead. We use to call them trolleys, but I was delighted to hear them referred to as 'bogies' by Danny Bligh's cousins from Bishop Auckland. It wasn't until the advent of television that I ever heard them called go-carts, but under pressure from those who would eradicate dialect (Mrs. Trout and Father McShame) the local names have disappeared and go-cart it is.

As I ferreted around in the back yard, my brothers arrived. Jack and Rodge were painted up like the Sioux braves we had seen in last week's picture 'Custer's Last Stand.' One of the rare occasions that Ned and Tim had been allowed to be the U.S. cavalry of course.

"What you doin'?" asked Ned.

"Making a trolley," I replied with a superior air considering the only progress I'd made was to find a hammer and a two-foot four-by-four.

"Great," said Ned. "We'll help." He and Tim relieved me of the hammer and the piece of wood and suddenly I was demoted from engineer to apprentice. But it soon became obvious that my brothers were seasoned scroungers and before the hour was out they had somehow acquired the plank for the body, a rope for steering, and a nut and bolt for the front axle.

"We need boolers," said Rodge.

"What's boolers?" I asked.

"Wheels, you broth head. And I think I know where we can get them." He left the yard and we followed him down to the top of Low Albion Street where we found Alice Dimpton and her suddenly interesting doll pram. Rodge conducted the negotiations.

"How much for your pram?" Smooth. Alice Dimpton wore one of her mother's long dresses that trailed along the ground and was filthy at the bottom. Her face was caked with make-up and her lips were buried under thick red lipstick. She was an only child and had a number of peculiarities, not the least of which was a habit of opening her eyes very wide and batting her lashes. Alice had once told her mother that she wanted to run away to the circus and, in order to avert that calamity, her mother had sent her to a drama class. Just the one, but it had lasting effects.

"Oh," she said with a swoon, sweeping a hand across her forehead. "How can I part with my precious pram?" Not bad for a nine-year-old. She made us all smile and you couldn't help but like her.

"Come on, Alice," said Rodge. "It's as old as the hills and I know you found it at the dump."

"Notwithstanding," she said. We looked at each other. None of us had heard that word before and I was sure she meant 'not worth sanding' so I told her we weren't interested in the quality of the paintwork. Then it was my turn to get stared at.

"Kiss, cuddle or torture?" she said suddenly. We froze. It was an offer every boy dreaded, but in the unspoken code of childhood, it was an offer you had to accept in one of its three modes. We all chose torture and were given a snake-burn to the wrist, the traditional reward for cowardice. Alice was disappointed, especially with Ned, whom she adored.

"Let's play skippy," she continued, magically producing a rope from the bottom of the pram. We steadfastly refused to skip rope, but Tim and I were obliged to hold the ends and twirl.

"Sing," said Alice.

"No."

"Sing or no pram."

Jack slapped the back of my head and I sang.

"On a mountain stands a lady who she is I do not know..."

"Everybody," said Alice. I smiled. Chorus:

All she wants is gold and silver all she wants is a nice young beau... Here came the tricky bit, she was about to select someone to skip with her. We just knew it was going to be Ned.

So come to me Neddy dear, Neddy dear, Neddy dear... she was delirious as Jack motioned Ned into the blur of rope and skipper. He skipped with illustrated reluctance, hands on hips and tongue tut-tut-tutting the whole time. I loved it. At the end of the refrain, Alice seemed well satisfied but still insisted we give her a shilling for the pram. Jack instructed us to empty our pockets and we duly obliged. In total we had the sum of sixpence. My sixpence. You may imagine how happy I was.

"We've only got a tanner," said Jack.

"Jus' right," replied Alice, and she took it from my hand, winked and exited stage left.

"Perfect," said Jack, turning the pram around. "Let's get it into the back yard and fix up the trolley." Off we went, back up the alley behind King Street and into the yard at number nineteen.

Much banging and sweating ensued, and at one point my dad returned home through the back gate and quizzed us about the noise.

"What are you lot up to?"

"Nothin, Dad," said Jack. "We're just making a trolley out of this old pram." The old man took a quick look around and seemed satisfied. Which was odd, because he almost never believed we could be doing anything that wasn't mischievous. I guessed he must have been preoccupied.

"If John-Robbie Chadfield comes by, tell him the meeting's at the bottom of High Queen Street at three o'clock this afternoon. And behave yourselves, right?"

"Right," we chimed. Then Dad disappeared again and we got back to work. We had removed the axles from the pram and stapled one to the plank and the other to the front-end and I sat down and swivelled the steering ropes to check out manoeuverability. By the time an hour had passed, the project was almost complete. It seemed perfect.

"One more thing," said Jack. "Let's put a box on it." He went to the washhouse and came out with a sturdy wooden box. On the side in large ornate letters it said 'Tizer Pop - Two Dozen.' Now, Dad had asked me earlier if I knew where that box was. If ever a thing went missing, I was always the first asked about it. So I knew for a fact that my dad wanted it to stand on when he addressed the good folks of the village later in the afternoon. But it was such a handsome box. And it would be the very dab for the trolley. So we nailed it down to the plank and stood back to admire our handiwork.

The trolley was a marvel to behold and we set out immediately for the old slagheap by the pigeon crees.

There was much squabbling about who got to ride, who pushed, who pulled. Jack sorted it all out by drawing straws. As usual, he somehow got the longest and rode in the trolley while the rest of us took turns to push. The hill we intended to substitute for Monte Carlo was a mountain of colliery slag piled there more than a hundred years earlier. It had grown over with whin and coarse grass, but there was a clear track down one side where the rain frequently washed away the topsoil. And this was to be the racetrack.

"O.K.," said Jack. "I'll go first to make sure it's safe." Who could argue? How brave of him. We positioned the trolley at the top of the hill and Jack stepped up to it. Before he got in he instructed the rest of us to watch him carefully as he was going to demonstrate how to cleverly turn the wheels on the way down, thus emulating a real racing car by skidding a bit from side to side. As he stepped on the edge of the box the trolley took off without him and he fell backwards as though he'd stepped on a banana skin. We weren't allowed to laugh out loud so I had to turn away. When I looked back the trolley was trundling through the bushes and heading away from the track at right angles towards the New Road. And coming down the New Road from the direction of Crook Town was a very large dump truck. It mashed into the trolley and sent it up into the air as high as a house. The truck didn't stop, but the driver was kind enough to stick his fingers up at us on the way past.

We rushed to the scene of the accident to find all our hard work had been reduced to a mess of mangled metal and splinters of wood. Every one of the boolers was buckled. The staples had all popped and the bolt had sheared. But the steering rope was fine, and, stuck in the lowest branch of a nearby hawthorn tree, the box had miraculously survived.

"Good job you weren't in it, eh?" I said to Jack to console him.

"It wouldn't have gone onto the road if I'd been in it. Was it you that pushed it too soon?" Charming, I thought. For my troubles, he made me drag the trolley back to the village. I got a first hand lesson in how much easier things became after the wheel was invented. As we rounded the corner of Queen Street, we bumped into a crowd gathering outside the cobbler's shop. Nutty Wicker was entertaining people while they waited for the main event, which of course was to be my dad's plea for unity in the face of bureaucratic contempt.

"Roll up, roll up," said Nutty. "Ladies and jellyfish, juveniles and crocodiles, come and witness what your eyes won't warrant." He was juggling an apple, a baby's bottle and a house brick. Pure magic. How could my dad possibly follow that? Crowds are like everything else to kids; subjected to time they tend to grow in the telling, but on this occasion I actually counted the people at the corner and there were twenty adults and a multitude of kids. One of the kids was Oswald MacDoogal, the five-year-old sweetheart of Witton Park on account of his having Down syndrome. Oswald was mimicking everything Nutty did and the two of them made quite a double act. By the time Dad stepped up to make his pitch, the whole throng was in a very merry mood.

"Thank you, Mr. Wicker," said my dad.

"Speak up, George!"

"Ah, yes. Well ..." and my dad looked around for his box. I just happened to have it handy. "Thanks, Son."

Some of the men who'd come out of the pub clapped and a couple of the women gave him a wolf-whistle. We shoved our way to the front of the crowd where my dad launched into a speech to rally the villagers to defend the inalienable rights of Britons not to be slaves.

"Why did we fight the war?" he implored. "Why did my brother lay down his life at Dunkirk except to keep us safe from life under the jackboot?" Not a bad start, but the crowd had heard this type of speech before. Like a thousand times during the war.

One on one, my dad could convince anyone to do anything for him. He had the personality and sincerity to carry the day. But for some reason, he was out of his depth up there on that box. And it didn't help that Oswald was standing right beneath him waving his arms and gesticulating every time my dad did. We thought it was hilarious and pretty soon the giggles started to escape from our mouths. Mine first of course. As my shoulders bobbed up and down, my dad shot me an almost fierce glare and I slunk back a row or two in the crowd. When I got it somewhat under control, I returned to listen to his alternatives to caving in to the whims of local government and his plan to make them renovate the village instead of destroying it.

It was interesting, and I believed him. But most of the people there were out of work and didn't own the houses they lived in anyway. They didn't much want to move, but they didn't much want to stay either. The end came unexpectedly early when the box on which my dad stood began to twist and buckle. The nails had split the wood in the accident and very, very slowly his feet disappeared into the box. Oswald pointed it out to those who had not immediately seen it, and at the finish everyone was laughing, including my dad.

As the crowd dispersed, I went to him and put my hand on his shoulder, the way he did to me whenever I failed at some task or other. He looked over at us and the beat up trolley.

"Oh, dear," he said. "Looks like you came a cropper. Never mind, lads, we tried, didn't we?" And then he turned around and scooped up Oswald in his arms.

"Come on, young 'un. I'll drop you off at your mother's." He lifted Oswald above his head and blew raspberries on his naked stomach, and the two of them went off along the street laughing hysterically.

The Cowboys

The noon sun (it was in fact 9:30 a.m.) beat mercilessly down upon the dusty cowboys. My older boys whistled incessantly at the imaginary steers while I could only manage the odd "git along there doggies," and other such bovine pleasers, as I was quite unable to produce anything remotely resembling a whistle. The week's offering at the cinema had been a western and its effect was being displayed across the great plains of the Wear valley. Bow-legged and slapping one rear cheek we rode the range rounding up strays and chasing off pesky coyotes.

Jack had a hat. It was wide brimmed and turned up at one side so that he looked a little like the debonair actor Stewart Granger, at least from the hairline up. Only a few hours earlier it had adorned a wooden headbust at the rear of a clothes closet in my mother's bedroom. Never having seen her wear it, he presumed (foolishly as he would later find) that it was of no use to her, and he had stripped it of its paisley headband, substituting in its place a red kerchief with white polka dots. Draped across his shoulder from left to right and down to his waist was his trusty lasso. This had been removed that morning from the nail behind the back kitchen door, thus ensuring no washing could be hung to dry in the fresh easterly wind that played through the village. How gay he looked! How very colonial! No wonder he remained unchallenged as the leader of our little fraternity.

"Mount up!" he cried, one hand raised above his head. We made horse-cum-cavalry noises and rode off obediently as he urged "Ho!" Tongues clicked rhythmically and experience told me that we were bound for the gill field to harass some poor cow, and more than likely sour her milk. No matter; how else was a boy to learn the indispensable art of steer roping?

Our way led westward, uphill to the top of Black Road; a place known as the Baltic. The village was filled with streets that carried the names of great victories and patriotic handles from its flourishing beginnings during the industrial revolution: Alma, Quebec, Trafalgar, Waterloo, Sudan; King Street, Queen Street, Coronation Terrace. On our left, starting at the ill-kempt edge of the presbytery garden, was a long wall just too high for a schoolboy to see over without jumping. It ran the length of the paddock where the Gypsies and hawkers kept their ponies, and it was the kind of thing boys simply had to walk along.

We climbed up according to the time-honoured custom of oldest to youngest. All went well until we reached the mid-point where a five-bar gate allowed access to the field. I climbed down and passed this obstacle on firm ground. The others, however, insisted on emulating the Amazing Blondin, inching across the top beam with arms spread wide. Jack, Roger and Ned made it over without trouble but Tim ... well, he would have made it had he not insisted on the pirouette half way. This not only unbalanced him but caused a burst of laughter that shot his concentration to pieces. Down he went and, accepting the inevitable, he clutched his heart and feigned a wound to make the bravest spectacle possible. I blasted a few holes in him by way of good measure and blew across the top of my finger to clear the smoke.

He landed in some newish horse-muck. Normally horse-muck is not so bad, but this nag must have had dysentery. The friends-and-brothers camaraderie went out of the window and Rodge and I kept

32

him at bay with sticks until he had scrubbed the offending leg with grass and the stink had subsided to a tolerable level.

Meanwhile, Jack was trying to put a rope around the gatepost. It was a seemingly easy target; after all it was four feet high and stationary. Try as he might, though, he couldn't lasso it. The problem seemed to lie in his not being able to whirl the rope in a manner that created a loop. Consequently when hurled at the post it remained limp and ineffective. I had to admire my eldest brother's vocabulary. He knew more Anglo-Saxonisms then than I do to this day.

"It's no use," he said. "It'll work better on real cows." Off we went. Oddly enough we actually believed him and went on to the meadow with an air of optimism.

The next hiccough to mar the outing occurred at the entrance to the gill field and it was at my expense. The style into the meadow was a rustic and ancient device that had been repaired at some time by the dairy farmer who was its main customer. By banging a pit prop straight down the centre of the old fence-wire he created a noble new portal that served two purposes…two-way traffic could use the style, and small boys could leapfrog the pit prop. When I, being somewhat wanting in the leg and voluminous in the pants, hurled myself skyward at the style, my trajectory fell somewhat short of the required minimum, resulting in a loud ripping noise and a sudden draught of cold air. My shorts—and thankfully nothing else—caught on the post and were ripped asunder, and I had to endure merciless pinches to my newly exposed backside.

Once again Jack set to work whirling the rope round and around to put a loop across the pit prop. As he slackened his grip on the spare folds of lariat, and the noose grew longer, he inadvertently (he said) lashed Roger across the top lip.

"Pigging Nora!" cried Rodge, holding his hand to his mouth as he rolled along the ground in agony. We laughed, of course, before helping him back to his feet and curiously examining the damage. Strangely, he looked quite good with this superimposed moustache and, on the advice of Jack, we all pressed the dirty rope on our top lips and tattooed on droopy growths. None of us looked nearly so good as Roger, as his stood proud of his face on top of the welt that the stinging rope had left. Too high a price for the authentic look, the rest of us decided, and contented ourselves by settling for the less

33

painful tidemark. We spent a few minutes calling each other Gringo and shouting *Arriba*, thinking these new acquisitions made us look more like caballeros than cowboys.

High clouds that rolled off the moors to the west billowed up like angel hair above the common. Occasionally, bright sun broke through and dappled the pretty patchwork of green fields, and at last we arrived at the gill field. This high grass was just good enough to graze cattle upon. Had it been a couple of hundred feet higher above sea level it would have sustained only sheep, but, as it stood, the milder growing months always hosted a herd of shorthorns and we lost no time in singling one out to star in our show.

Unfortunately this uncooperative bullock guessed our intentions and in his panic spooked the entire herd. The cattle ran around in disarray whenever any of us approached. It was frustrating to say the least. Didn't they know we'd come a long way to practice roping? Or did they not care to cooperate? It seemed the latter was true. Jack was most put out. With a sudden superiority he told the rest of us, "*Cush* is what you say to call cows. Kit Carson told me," Kit Carson was a local farm labourer, not *the* Kit Carson of Western movies fame. "Cush! Cush! Come on now, I won't hurt you." The cows did not believe him either and took off without exception the moment the rope was whirled.

"Herd them over here," Jack instructed, and we tried to comply, running about with our arms flailing the air, crying *Cush* and *Gertcha*. At this point big brother began to grow impatient, blaming each failure on one or other of us. Mostly me. We persevered for over half-an-hour, but in the end had to concede defeat and reluctantly we plodded back, red-faced, panting and sweating, up the grassy slope to the top of the field and climbed the style. No one bothered to leap it. It had all been such a let down. We leaned against the dry stone wall and gazed back at the cattle.

"The buggers are laughing at us!" exclaimed Ned. They did seem to be wearing a kind of smirk.

"We could try Friesians," suggested Roger, half-heartedly. By the look on Jack's face he was in no mood to try again. For a few minutes we exchanged glances with the cows, some of us chewing straws, some of them chewing the cud, until Jack turned away and in doing so silently motioned us to follow. Tim stooped and picked up a stone.

"If you hit 'em on one of their horns it goes curly and they drop dead," he said. Sometimes I wondered how he thought them up. In a sour grapes gesture he wound up and loosed the stone at one of the shorthorn bullocks. It missed.

Retracing our steps we again climbed the wall and, though at first hushed and stunned, we were soon back to our usual chattering, happy selves. Coming up the wall from the village was Beaker, the village snitch.

"Guess what?" he implored. No one bit and he went on, "We're moving to Aycliffe!"

"Great," said Jack. "The sooner the better." And he pushed Beaker off the wall without ceremony. We each blew him a raspberry as we passed.

"You can come and visit me, Philip," he said, but I didn't look back and we trooped on toward the village.

Across the adjacent road, just where the gate was, stood a tiny shop belonging to Mrs. Longstop. Although none of us had money to spend, we climbed down and peered through the window. There we lusted a while at the acres of confectionery before taking a detour around the back of the house to see the litter of pigs that had recently been produced by Bertha, Mrs. Longstop's champion sow. They were by that time well used to being stared at, even if they were just a week old, for every kid within a mile had been by to give them the once over. Well, pigs are very dear to a boy's heart, aren't they?

Sadly, the mother had squashed one of the piglets and it lay lifeless at one end of the pen. We took hold of some pea-canes and tried to retrieve the corpse. Bertha was having none of it and, baring her great yellow teeth, she charged the chicken-wire fence and barked loudly. We took off instantly. Pigs don't like small boys. Pigs and cows.

By the time we stopped running we were in Park Terrace, a short row of mean houses that leaned together for support at the top of the village, themselves just south of the overworked garden allotments. All in all it hadn't been much of a morning, and we consoled ourselves by making current sandwiches. This entailed encasing wild currants, the earliest berry to ripen, in sour docks, small leaves of ground-growing sorrel with surprisingly good astringency. I was a sight! It was not often that I thought so myself, but on this occasion, with the crotch of my khaki shorts dangling between my grass-stained knees, and a purple berry stain around my mouth, it could not be denied. Ensuing attempts to clean up my phizzog only served to spread the juice over an even greater area. Still, I had tried.

As we were homeward bound, informed by internal clocks that lunchtime was fast approaching, we took a short cut to our house on King Street by using the Wickets. This was a narrow footpath that connected Park Terrace with the rest of the village, bisecting at one point the lower section of Black Road. As we reached this point, Jack held up a hand and we all stopped. Somewhere in the distance I could hear the faint piggy-piggy-piggy of a small motorcycle and, to my astonishment, my brother unfurled the lasso and began to whirl it around his head.

Now, there exists a law somewhere that states that 'if a thing can possibly happen, it will.' It might be noted that where we were concerned a further premise could be added, 'its occurrence is directly proportional to the trouble it will cause.' I don't know who came up with that particular gem, but it is undoubtedly accurate. The odds against the rope forming a loop at all had been demonstrated to be infinitesimally minute; it followed that the chances of actually roping anything were non-existent. Jack let fly as the tiny post-office motorbike chugged by. Not even the postman was more shocked than we when the lariat slipped over his shoulders and tightened around his torso. Two seconds later the poor man was sitting on his arse in the middle of the road while his bike continued on its way. Eyes popped; jaws hit the ground. Jack held on to the rope only until the disbelief in his eyes met the terror in the dazed postie's. As the full extent of the situation hit home we turned tail and, after initially panicking into one and other in chaos, we fled.

It was quite some time before we dared go home, thinking the whole episode would have been relayed to our parents via mystic radar; that inscrutable talent mothers have for knowing things you rather they didn't. By some strange quirk of fate, the man on the bike had not reported the transgression. Perhaps he had sat and thought about it and decided that it had not really happened. Or perhaps he had decided that he could not handle the ribbing he would get from his mates at the sorting station. Anyway, the list now reads cows, pigs and postmen.

At The Hop

It was the night of the 'Sweethearts Ball,' a wartime invention intended to give young lovers a last night together before the boy was sent off as cannon fodder and the girl was subjected to the rigors of factory life. It met with such success that it was continued for younger teenagers long after the war ended. There were no soldiers in the village by that time, and the days of National Service had ended. But the dance at the laughably misnamed village hall (we called it 'the hut') continued to attract all the young bravados and the girls from far and wide.

Each year, they made a special effort to torture themselves into clothes too tight and too ridiculous for words.

"Puttin' on the agony, puttin' on the style," sang my dad as he'd watched the teenagers troop past the house on the way to the hall. *"That's what all the young folk are doin' all the while."* Mother, for some reason, went quite gooey. She smiled the broadest smile and linked her arm through his, whispering things and making him smile too.

Danny Bligh and myself had walked to the hall right at the beginning of the dance, even before the girls had begun to hit the floor. Tim, Ned and Rodge were there before us. So too, more surprisingly, was Beaker. As minors were not normally welcomed to grown-up events like the dance, we were obliged to hang around in the shadows outside, peeking through the cracks in doorframes to see what was going on.

"Cor," said Danny. "Nancy Rollings!" Nancy looked like a composite of all the Hollywood starlets. Even my dad looked at her when she passed, and he was almost forty. She was the first to take to the floor with her friend Alison, who was what my mother called 'wholesome' and what the older boys called 'ugly.' They stood stock-still as the first bars from Bill Haley filled the room:

One, two, three o'clock, four o'clock rock!
Five, six, seven o' clock, eight o' clock rock!
Nine, ten, eleven o'clock twelve o'clock rock!
We're gonna rock around the clock tonight...

...and only then did these two begin to bop. Inside, the older boys stood around the perimeter of the dance hall and pretended not to be bothered with the goings-on of the dancers. It was cool to be uninterested. But outside, in the dust of the evening, we considered the performance a treat indeed.

The hut had been hurriedly built without the luxury of a foundation, consequently it stood on pilings and the floor inside was two feet higher than ground level. As we were somewhat short, we were able to look right up the girl's skirts when they whirled around. Worth waiting a year for. No panty hose then—just the seamed stockings and suspender belts of our dreams. And we watched in silence as the crinoline skirts flared out at the end of every verse and chorus. I wondered what it was exactly that was so good about this ritual, why it made me feel so strange. Of course I never asked. And I somehow don't think any of the boys with me could have supplied an answer.

At the end of the first song, the air seemed even quieter than usual and we became aware of the natural noises of the night.

"Do you hear them?" said Beaker.

"No."

"Listen, shh..."

Behind the hut a breeze whined through the knotted fingers of the poplar trees. High overhead a convincing whisper persistently hissed.

"A tree was planted for every lad who died in the war," Beaker said. "An' on this night every year, they call for their mothers and sweethearts."

"What a load of crap," said Tim. "It's the wind, you idiot." Tension thus relieved, giggles erupted and I felt better. Roger placed his finger on Beaker's chest then ran it up his face when he looked down. The older boys smacked his ears, blew raspberries and sent him on his way. When he was a safe distance off, he looked back at me.

"You jus' listen, Philip."

"Get lost, Beaker," I said. And Beaker left.

"Pigging Nora!" cried Ned, startling us all. "Look who spinning the discs!" We cranked our necks to look toward the right hand end of the dance hall, and to our combined amazement we saw Jack

38

sitting with Lloyd Foster at the turntable. Well, I can't tell you in what esteem disc jockeys were held in those days. About on a par with God I suspect, except on dance night when the man with the music reigned supreme. Lloyd Foster was fifteen and much sought after as the owner of the loudest record player in the village. He knew expressions like *yowsa* and *you're in the groove, Jackson* and used them at precisely the right time.

Jack's hair was plastered to his head with Brylcreem and he shone like a bullfighter. He was wearing one of Lloyd's Teddy Boy suits and the skinniest tie in the world. The suit was far too big for him, but someone (Lloyd's mother I expect) had done a fix-up job and somehow he looked like he belonged in there. No wonder he was my hero.

"Let's see if he can get us in," said Danny. Obviously Danny didn't know Jack as well as we did.

"He won't be very pleased if we show him up," I said. The others agreed, and we decided to watch him and the girls from the safety of the shadows. More and more 16 year-old 'men' were showing up. They had been to the pub to buy Dutch courage in the form of brown ale, and now they were here; all swank and suave. Well, they thought so. We did.

The record player was state-of-the-art. It was a foot square and the lid had to be removed to get the disc onto the turntable. The lid also held the four-inch speaker that was cranked to blast the hall in six-watt splendour.

"Hey!" came a rough voice. "Short arse! Play some Pat Boone." No mistaking that request. But, as I learned from Jack later, no one in their right mind was playing Pat Boone those days—*it don't mean a thing if it ain't got dat swing*—and the refusal to spin it was based on a sound professional judgment. Good taste in music, but poor judge of large humans. They selected instead the latest from Cliff Richard - *The Young Ones*. The floor filled immediately with teenagers and Lloyd flashed a told-you-so glance at Jack.

Those were the days of the three-minute song and it was over before the dud dancers had time to quit or be abandoned out on the dance floor. Tom Coglan, the Pat Boone fan, was again at the stage requesting his song. He sat back down next to Sandra Colville and offered her a cigarette that she declined. Sandra turned fourteen two weeks before and sat plastered in foundation that looked like it had been applied with a trowel. She was one class ahead of Jack at school and was always asking me about him.

"When exactly is his birthday? How old did you say?" I wondered why an old woman wanted to know so many dumb things and why she didn't just ask him herself. Coglan's face dropped when Chuck Berry took the crowd across the ocean to Memphis, Tennessee. The outside crew forgot the DJs for two minutes and thirty-five seconds while we gorged ourselves on visual delights.

"Nellie Best's wearing pink ones!" Frenzied rush to Danny's spy-hole. When the song was finished, Coglan was wagging his finger in Lloyd's face. He wasn't happy.

"I want my gramophone record played, right?" Then he sat back down and said something to Sandra and they both stood up and joined the expectant revellers all ready and waiting out on the floor.

> *On a day like today*
> *We'll pass the time away*
> *Writing love letters in the sand...*

Except for Coglan and Sandra, the entire crowd returned to their chairs. A moan audible over the crooner went around and a couple of people even booed. Coglan held onto Sandra and continued to dance. She didn't look so comfortable to me, leaning up and in on tiptoes to whisper in his ear. He shook his head at her and scowled. Then she cast an imploring look toward the stage and mouthed the word 'help.' Lloyd looked up at the nicotine-coated ceiling and began to whistle along with the song. I sympathised with Sandra. This slow stuff was no good at all for twirling dance partners.

When I looked at my eldest brother I saw a look on his face that I had never seen before. Hard to describe, really. Kind of wet. His eyebrows were raised and drooped at the same time, so he looked a bit like a very old dog. He reached out his hand and pulled the arm of the record player so Pat Boone ended with an abrupt er-r-r-r-up! A cheer from some of the boys was followed by a silence. Coglan turned around and stared toward the stage.

"I need a leak, man. Got to, like, split," said Lloyd, and he disappeared through the curtain at the side of the stage. Jack sat still and tried to look cool. Total failure. His knees began to wobble and he held on to the table for support.

"I think we better get in there an' help," I said. The others looked at me as though I was mad.

"He's sixteen," said Tim. "He'll kill us."

"Oh, yeah. I forgot."

Coglan climbed onto the stage with a single stride and took hold of Jack by the ear. He pulled him to the edge and gave him a kick in the pants so that he fell off the stage and onto the dance floor.

"Stay down!" Coglan commanded him. Now, if it had been me, I would have stayed down. In fact, there was only one person I could think of whose pride would not allow him to do so. And there he was on the floor. He got to his knees and Coglan jumped off the stage and booted him in the stomach.

"I said, stay down!"

"He's only twelve," said Sandra. "Leave him alone."

"Who asked you? Mind yer own business."

"I said, leave him alone," she repeated.

"Oh, yeah? What are you gonna do about it?" And, at Coglan's expense, every boy inside and outside the dance hall learned a lesson on the consequences of not respecting women. Sandra lifted her knee sharply into his groin and he went down like a sackful of chisels. Another cheer from the crowd. And one from us outside. Sandra helped Jack to his feet and toward the door.

"I think we'd better go," she said. They stepped out into the foyer of the hut and through the door. We pretended to be doing things like inspecting the paint in the dark, and checking the walls of the hut. You know, natural stuff.

"What are you little buggers doing? Looking up skirts?" How could she possibly have known that?

"Of course not," said Rodge. "We were waiting for Jack."

"Well he's coming home with me." They linked arms and turned away from us.

"He's not twelve anymore," I called. "He was thirteen las' week."

"I know," she said, quietly. And the shadows swallowed them as they walked off towards the railway yard.

"Let's go before Coglan comes out," said Rodge. And we obeyed the second-in-command and headed back toward King Street.

It had been a strange night; full of bits of things that wouldn't fit together. It didn't sit right that Jack had let Sandra Colville link his arm. And for the life of me I didn't see why they had to walk home by the railway yard. It was black as night there and they'd never be able to see a thing. Why did Beaker have to say such a stupid thing about the treetops? Would those dead men still call when the houses were flat and their mothers and sweethearts had all moved away? And who would be there to listen?

The Best Laid Plans

I imagine the arrival of the black plague was greeted with about the same amount of blah as the first gaggle of surveyors that arrived in Witton Park on that crisp May morning. I remember it so well because as I was on my way to school Jennifer Mountjoy's mother called me over and asked me to take her daughter along. I could have died.

Mrs. Mountjoy had just moved to the village to take care of her sick aunt, Mrs. Bell. I had never seen old Mrs. Bell as she had been bed-ridden since time out of mind. To me she existed only as a phantom behind the permanently drawn drapes of the downstairs window at number six High Thompson Street. She was a source of dread to kids on our street, and the very last thing you wanted to do was go into that dim house that always smelled of eucalyptus.

"Hello, Philip," said Mrs. Mountjoy. "Jennifer is almost ready and I'd be very glad if you would take her to school this week till she knows her way around." It probably never occurred to her that her daughter was a girl. And I was a boy. Was she mad or something? I absolutely could not do this thing.

"O.K.," I said.

"Come in to the warm," she said.

"Crikey... I mean, er, no thanks. I'll just wait here if that's all right."

"I'll give you a slice of toast an' jam while you wait." What a dilemma. And how cruel to make a kid choose between the evil eye and a slab of jammy toast. Mrs. Mountjoy disappeared for a minute and came back with a hefty doorstep of freshly toasted bread veritably dripping with raspberry jam. No contest.

"Ta, Missus." And I was across the threshold like something bewitched. Mrs. Mountjoy went off to get Jennifer ready and as I

42

polished off the toast I looked around. I was surprised to find the inside of the house structured exactly like my own.

Old Mrs. Bell had photographs all over the hallway and a flight of plaster ducks was on its perpetual migration up the stairwell. The pictures were all of grim-looking people with ne'er a smile between them. The men all had beards and the women wore pinched expressions. I wondered how anyone could ever have loved them enough to put their pictures on the wall. Maybe they were there to frighten children. In which case they were good pictures.

The most remarkable of the photos was just inside the front room, where the invalid lay in wait for me. It had been purposefully placed there, I thought, to lure innocents to their doom. It was an image of Mr. Bell, dead since the battle of the Somme in the Great War. One of the poplar trees at the south of the village had been planted in his memory. Mrs. Bell would have the double misfortune of living long enough to see the tree destroyed with almost the same disregard that had swept her man from the earth.

In the picture he was regaled in all the paraphernalia of regimental splendour - dress uniform with tons of buttons and lanyards hanging everywhere. He stood at the 'stand easy' mode with a rifle at his side and what looked like hand grenades of some kind around his belt. All wonderful stuff for giving what-for to troublesome natives around the empire. What a shock it must have been to take on the Hun and find out the buggers fought back.

Show-stopping though the uniform was, it was Mr. Bell himself that was most fascinating. He was a massive man. Taller than his horse, he dwarfed everything in the photograph. His chest was wide enough to bear the medals of a hundred campaigns, and it did. His neck was a wondrous thing to behold and spilled over the stiff collar with muscle to spare. And his moustache was waxed into wings that even Lord Kitchener would have envied.

"Come in, young man," said a tiny clear voice. Ice formed on the back of my neck and I considered making a run for it. But a morbid curiosity forced me to look around and into the eyes of Mrs. Bell. She looked exactly like Miss Haversham in Great Expectations. I know, because I saw the movie at the picture-house three weeks earlier.

"I'll not bite you," she said, but I wasn't sure. And neither was I sure what it actually was that she did to kids, except that it must be pretty awful because Jack always opened his eyes really wide when he talked about her— "Mrs. Bell lives in the dark."—how could you not have the willies after that?

"Would you like a mint imperial?" she said. Several things crossed my mind, like is it poisoned… are there pins in it… has she had it in her mouth already? But of course I had zero in the way of self-discipline and my hand went out towards her as I watched in horror. She slipped me a mint and I placed in on my tongue and kissed my life goodbye.

After I didn't die I became relatively comfortable with the situation and found to my pleasure that the old lady was quite nice. When she laughed she showed pink gums and a slight wheeze in her giggle reminded me of my own granny. From somewhere under the bedding she produced two more crumpled paper bags and held one in either hand.

"Dainty Dinah? Black bullet?" she offered. I crunched the mint in my mouth and went for one of each. The black bullets were stuck together and I was a bit embarrassed that a lump of about six came out.

"That's all right," she said. "Dainty Dinah?" They were a particular favourite of mine and my mother used them to bribe me on occasion. I'd do almost anything to get one of these toffees. And here was Mrs. Bell giving me one for nothing. I was suspicious, but not enough to put me off.

"Ta, missus." And I slipped the goodies into my pocket so that I could pull them out later, smack my lips before dropping them into my mouth one at a time, and thereby torture the kids at school.

The old woman pulled the quilt closer about herself and smiled like a little girl. She looked me up and down just as I examined her. I'd never seen a bed cap, except in pictures. Hers was made of lace, exquisitely embroidered with tiny posies of fanciful flowers. Her hands were small like a child's and I couldn't make out the outline of a body at all under the white linen nightgown. If it wasn't for her wrinkled face, you'd think she was about nine years old.

"What's your name?"

"Philip."

"And where do you live, Philip?"

"King Street. Number nineteen."

She got this vacant look in her eyes and was quiet for a while. I could hear the clock out in the hall marking time with its painfully slow ticking. I wondered what was taking Mrs. Mountjoy so long to get Jennifer ready and who Dainty Dinahs were named after.

"Have you always lived there?" she suddenly asked.

"Yes," I said. "Except for when I was born in Sedgefield. I lived in the hospital for a week." She smiled and I smiled with her. I told her that we'd be moving to Newton Aycliffe when the houses came down, and that by coincidence today the men from the council were walking around with telescopes on poles, writing things in books as they went. I told her that my dad had said we'd all have to move away and how he was pretty mad about that 'cos they never asked his opinion and who did these little Hitlers think they were anyway.

"Now then, Philip," said Mrs. Mountjoy who had come into the room with Jennifer. "Mother doesn't want to hear that kind of talk. Here's Jennifer. Off you go!" And she bustled the pair of us outside in somewhat of a hurry. I turned to say goodbye but she just tut-tutted and closed the door on us.

"What did I do?" I said.

"You mustn't talk to Gran about the house," said Jennifer. "She cries when she sees the letter from the council and Mam sez she'll not be coming to Canada with us."

"You're going to Canada, not Aycliffe?"

"Yes."

"Where'll she go, then?"

"She's going to a home in Sunderland. Nuns will look after her, Mam sez. She'll like that. She a bit batty y'know."

"Yeah," I agreed. "She gave me Dainty Dinahs for nothing."

I began to walk away when I heard this tiny cough behind me. I looked around and Jennifer was wearing an indignant expression and her arm was extended.

"You'll have to hold my hand," she said. "I don't want to get lost." I smiled. I knew this must be some kind of a joke. But her face was quite still and her hand remained outstretched.

I thought and thought for over a minute. When I turned to walk away she began to cry and she looked just like her grandmother. I looked around to see if anyone was watching. The street was empty except for way down the bottom two men with surveyor's poles were unwinding the longest tape measure I'd ever seen.

"Shall they pull Granny's house down today?" she asked.

"Of course not," I said. "Come on. But you let go as soon as we see anybody."

We wended our way up Black Road at a dawdling pace so that we would not catch up to the other kids and I would not be seen holding Jennifer's hand. At Mrs. Longstop's shop we detoured and walked behind the houses until we got to the junction with Baltic Terrace. I peeked carefully around the corner.

"Won't we be late?" asked Jennifer.

"Mebbe."

At nine sharp Mrs. Trout walked out onto the playground and jangled the brass school bell. I imagined the kids running to line up for class.

"It's the bell!" said Jennifer in panic. She gave a tug at my hand but I was having none of it. I'd far rather risk being late than suffer the jibes of my pals if they knew I'd escorted a girl to school. I counted the agonising minutes until I thought everyone would be inside school, then I hauled a surprised Jennifer into the open and made a bolt across the road. Once across, I let go of her hand and shoved her through the girl's gate. It was cruel but what could I do? I ran around to the boy's entrance and just tagged on to the tail end of the queue.

"Nearly late, Philip," said Mrs. Trout, in a disapproving tone.

"Nearly, Miss."

After morning prayers we all sat down on the class-wide benches behind the long wooden desks. It was Monday and the first lesson was to be composition. Normally the pencils were given out by Beaker, who was at the front of the class ready and waiting. He looked at Mrs. Trout with cocker spaniel eyes and a sickening, goofy expression. Just then the door opened from the infant class and Miss Macardle, the headmistress, walked in with Jennifer Mountjoy in tow. I just knew it meant trouble.

"Good morning, Standard One."

The whole class stood up and replied with the usual greeting.

"Good morning, Miss Macardle."

"This is a new girl who will be with us for a while. Her name is Jennifer Mountjoy," then she turned to Beaker and broke his heart. "William, I think today we'll let Philip hand out the pencils." Beaker

46

sat down, devastated, and I looked on in disbelief. The headmistress beamed at me.

"Philip was kind enough to bring Jennifer to school this morning," she said. All my pals turned to look at me. I was beet-red. Could this really be happening? What had I done to deserve this? I could not imagine that anyone ever in the history of time had been as embarrassed as I was at that moment. Surely it could get no worse.

"And," she went on. " Jennifer tells me he held her hand the whole way."

The Fishing Expedition

"Where are you going?" I asked. Tim and Ned were busy packing a haversack with odds and sods and it all looked very exciting.

"We'll probably need this," said Tim, putting a flat iron into the bag. "You never know."

"Where are you going?" I said again. Knives, tin plates, sandwiches with bizarre fillings encased in waxed bread wrappers, string, a pop bottle filled with (alas) water...

"Where are you going?"

...more string, a towel...

"Where are you going?"

"Fishing," said Ned, "Get lost!"

"Can I come?"

"No."

"Please!"

"Pathetic," said Tim. "Why don't you get lost? You're not coming." Never having learned to take no for an answer, I set about gathering my own gear together, determined to accompany them, welcome or not. It was always the same, they said no, but I'd tag along anyway. They ignored me for a while but eventually let me join in. That's what being a little brother entails.

Rushing from the house I rejoined them in the back yard and stood wide eyed and breathless in the sunshine; nylon net in one hand, gleaming jam-jar in the other. They returned my gaze with open-mouthed looks of scorn, followed by a gale of laughter and a pile of ridicule.

47

"What's that?" said Tim sarcastically.

"We're going proper fishing," added Ned in an equally scathing manner. "Not kid's stuff, *proper*." They laughed and jeered but I took no notice.

Upon opening the back gate we were met with the ready waiting figure of Alan Jimson, who always failed to see the funny side of anything. He was dressed as usual in a Sloppy-Joe tee-shirt and khaki shorts. His mother always turned him out in a white tee-shirt but it never stayed that way long. I could never fathom why she gave him a fresh one every day when it would obviously get mucked up.

"What's he doing here? He's not coming," said Alan. A fine hello, I thought. I showered him with praise and hero worship, but he really was not very pleased at all.

"Every time your brother comes with us something goes wrong," he said to the older boys. He was not entirely in error. One or two odd things had happened while I was present. Like the time the tree we were climbing suddenly succumbed to Dutch elm disease and the branch he was on plummeted to the ground. His arm broke in three places. Or that time we went camping. Alan was standing minding his own business when the head of the hatchet I was using to bang in tent pegs came off the shaft and flew through the air at lightening speed. The blunt side smashed him right between the eyes and they both went black. The lump that came up was like a bullfrog's throat. He was convinced that I was a jinx and nothing could shake him from his belief.

Fortuitously, his insistence that I was bad news prompted my brothers to stick up for me. After all, it may have been true, but it was not for an outsider to observe, and as they could not stand up for family honour and banish me to the house at the same time, the fishing trip was on. Within minutes we were under way.

"We'll go to the Eureka first," Alan said, "So we'll have some bait to fish with." The Eureka was the remnants of what had once been a park, it had once been landscaped with plants but had reverted to a wild state: current bushes, some privet. They looked forlorn and not a bit as their long dead planters had planned. There, too, was the concrete and brick plinth that had held the gazebo that was the village bandstand. Summerhouse and band were long gone and the whole area was frequented only by the secretive thrushes and blackbirds that searched for snails and grubs.

The place fascinated me, especially when I was alone. I fancied it was haunted by ghosts of soldiers dressed in strange and bright tunics; brass buttons gleaming as they danced under summer stars with ladies in long crinoline gowns, faces hidden behind gossamer fans. The vision would vanish as the grey English sky washed the land and the silence was quite eerie, but as such apparitions never appear before witnesses, I did not mind being there at all that day.

"Lift the stones and grab the worms!" was the simple instruction from Alan. The weather had been unusually mild and the earth was bone dry. Not a single worm was found, though we searched earnestly for almost a half hour. At the turn of what must have been the last unchecked stone, a centipede raced across its surface and began to run up my arm at a rapid rate of knots. Tim, who happened at that moment to be holding the bamboo fishing net, cried:

"Look out! Hundred legger!" Without hesitation, he slashed at it with gritted teeth and grim determination. He missed the centipede but caught me a good 'un. The whack with the whippy wand produced an instant welt and sent an all but unbearable pain searing through me. I lost no time in conveying this fact to the world.

The sharpness of the sting subsided and glowing warmth spread along the top of my forearm. The others wore grins, none more obvious than Alan Jimson, which, as I recall, I found most annoying. Boys will be boys, however, and, had the roles been reversed, I must admit that I would have found it difficult not to snigger a little. The flash of anger disappeared with the hurt and I laughed along with them, a move that once and for all made me one of the gang.

"Well then," began Ned, "What do we use for bait now?" The question stumped us all for a while.

"Wasp grubs are good." Alan said absently, for in his heart he knew that none of us much fancied suffering dozens of wasp stings just to go fishing. (Although I have it on good authority that some do.) Then his eyes widened as if he had suddenly remembered something, and he turned and ran towards home.

"I'll be back in five minutes!" he cried over his shoulder.

"Where's he going?" asked Ned.

"Dunno," I said. We awaited his return by the roadside and engaged in some game that involved the use of the fishing rods as swords. To my astonishment, Tim managed to slash me again in the exact same spot as before, with much the same effect, only now I was marked with a cross, which I thought looked quite good, and almost worth it.

"Excalibur!" Tim explained. I never knew what that meant but it sounded great and was entirely satisfactory. Ned took out the water-filled pop bottle and we each took a swig. We ate the sandwiches—we had after all been on the road for more than forty minutes—and drank again. Soggy bits of crumb shot up into the bottle as each of us drank till eventually there seemed to be as much chewed bread in the bottle as there was water.

Alan Jimson returned, out of breath and holding a tin box embossed with the single word 'Oxo', trademark of his mother's favourite brand of bouillon cubes.

"Gravy!" I blundered, "Fish don't eat gravy!" I was the only one laughing and I discovered why when I looked back at the box and saw it with its lid open displaying an array of beautifully coloured spinners and spoons and plugs.

"Oh!" I said, quietly. We all gazed into the tin, awe-struck at the loveliness of the little trout lures that flashed like spangles of gold and silver in some pirate's chest. Each took one to examine more closely, although it seemed irreverent to do so.

"They're my dad's," explained Alan "He'll kill me if he finds out I've nicked 'em." Only he cared. The rest of us couldn't wait to rig them up and have at the piscine population of the local river. Those who angle may cringe to know that none of us at that time had any notion of swivels, leaders, landing nets, or disgorgers, and on reflection our assault on the ecology of County Durham was not far short of criminal.

"You'll not be needing one," said Alan, without emotion, "They're only for proper rods." My heart sank as he snatched the Devon minnow from my hand. By way of consolation he tossed me the blade of a broken pike spoon. It was greeny-yellow with red polka dots. I loved it at once.

"Can I keep it?" I asked this with baited breath, fully expecting to be told no, so it was a very pleasant surprise when he replied,

"All right. It's busted anyway." I slipped it into the right pocket of my khaki shorts (the left had a hole in it) and skipped for joy for some yards before deciding that only little kids did that. Still, despite its having no use to him, I took the gift as a great compliment and decided to try my very best never to annoy Alan again.

"Let's get cracking!" cried Ned, and we eagerly trooped off toward the water.

As we entered the wood that cloaked the river, all went very quiet and the contrast between the cool shade beneath the leafy canopy and the warm sunshine of the open meadow was quite sharp. Bluebells were the denizens of this dim world and the smell of wild garlic was everywhere. Occasionally birds, mostly fat woodpigeons, would burst from their hiding places with a suddenness that startled, and we couldn't resist having a quick scout about to try and locate their nests. No one seemed bothered that birds had abandoned their nests long since.

The earth grew darker and was even boggy in places, especially where cattle had left deep hoof-prints along the narrow paths that they used on the occasions when maddening thirst drove them to the riverbank to drink. We had once been thrilled to discover the bloated body of one parched cow that had toppled in and lost its life in the ensuing struggle to escape. The water there was sluggish and deep, even during dry spells when the flow higher up and further downstream was virtually non-existent. The flowing green moss under the surface looked dark and forbidding.

"Peg Powler will getcha if you go too close..." Alan said. Peg was the mythical river witch who grabbed unsuspecting children and dragged them to their death when they strayed near the water. We hurried away.

Unexpectedly, the trees thinned and a shaft of sunlight lit a grassy patch of bank-side about twenty feet long, edged by tall rosebay willow herb and giant fronds of angelica in full bloom. The earthy smell of onion was replaced by subtle aroma of anise. We inspected the surface of the water. It was glass-flat and liberally speckled with leaves and fallen flower heads. Water-boatmen sculled themselves to and fro, and whirligig beetles performed their crazed dance a few inches from the bank. A thousand flies buzzed and bobbed just above the water; now and then dipping their feet below the surface as if to tease the fish. Indeed, had we but known, no self-respecting trout had eaten anything other than flies since mid-May. Nothing was going to show an interest in the imitation minnows with which we were about to flail the water, and that, I think, compensated quite adequately for the clumsy approach we made.

Now came the moment of truth. The older boys began to tackle up. Twelve-pound line (sturdy stuff, this) threaded though the guides and tied directly to the spoons without ceremony. Bail arms open, slowly back, and ...whiz! How good they looked as they flew through the air, and what a magnificent splash at the end of it all! Every fish for a quarter of a mile must have all but died of fright when the spinners hit the water. They spluttered and popped along the surface as they were speedily retrieved. I doubt very much whether a fish would have been quick enough to catch one of the treble hooks even if they had looked tempting, which they decidedly did not.

Meanwhile, I had walked to the end of a large log that jutted out into the river. Below it shone the silver bellies of the gambolling minnows, darting in unison first one way, then another. Cautiously I dipped my net into the river. They disappeared at once. I withdrew the net. They re-appeared.

"Mus' be a trick of the light," I thought. "I wonder if they'd like this?" I fumbled in my pocket for the blade. Carefully placing it in the bottom of the net, I lowered it into the shoal of fish. Again they disappeared but returned a few seconds later, in a great ball, to inspect the lure. Many were brave enough to take a bite at it, and within seconds it was almost completely obscured by a writhing, swirling mass of fish! Quick as a wink I hauled the net from the water. To my delight it contained a dozen or so 'pin heads, ' and one fat minnow, shining blue and red in his metallic breeding colours. Him I deposited into my jam jar whilst the others were dumped back into the river, none the worse for their little adventure. Soon I had increased the captive population to three, all male, and all decked out in their gaudy woo-ing garb.

The afternoon wore on, and I enjoyed this pleasant pursuit enormously. Behind me, the boys were having no luck at all, nothing bit, except the midges, and from the regular outburst of profanities that came from them, I guessed that their patience was wearing thin. Maybe they'd like to see some real fish? Proudly I held up my jar and walked across the piles of driftwood and jetsam until I stood a short way behind them.

"How do you like my catch?" I asked, rather haughtily. They turned as one and before I realised what was happening they were all over me.

"Great!" said Ned. He took the string handle and held up my jar.

"Jus' what we need!" added Alan, "Gimme one!" Then, before my eyes, they tipped the minnows out onto the grass and each grabbed one. I was too bewildered to guess the next move, and too naive to know that it would be so horrific. Following the lead of Alan Jimson, they impaled the little fish on the tri-pronged hooks and flung them, still alive, far out into the river. My mouth was wide open and my jar was empty.

"Pigging heck!" I cried, "What did you do that for?" Tim looked at me with surprised expression.

"Well, that's what they're for you know. Anyway, they can't feel pain, anybody knows that!" Somehow this didn't console me at all, although I remember I was glad that they weren't suffering. That they felt no pain was a myth I believed for many years afterward. Some people still believe it, and that if you pick dandelions you'll wet the bed, and if you turn thrice about at midnight on Halloween you'll see the wind. Anyone knows that only pigs can see the wind.

Well, the live bait worked no better than the lures, and we were about to call it a day. I was pretty peeved at my fish being destroyed, as by now they were well and truly on their way to that great eddy in the sky, so I said to Alan, nicely, so as not to annoy him:

"I think you should let me have a go at casting," he looked at me sideways, and I went on, "After all, you killed my minnows didn't you? I mean you did, didn't you?" Reluctantly he agreed.

"All right, but only one cast, an' if you lose the lure you go in an' get it. My dad'll murder me if he finds out I used his gear!" I agreed to the terms and eagerly took the fibreglass rod from him. Deftly I stepped to river's edge and, trying to copy all I had seen the others do, (for in truth this was my first attempt at casting, although I assured Alan that I was quite proficient) I lifted the bail arm and peeled off a few loops of mono-filament. Then I leaned back and, closing my eyes, gave a mighty heave and hoped for the best. I looked out over the water awaiting the splash of the spoon but none came. Instead, there was an astonished cry from behind me.

"Pigging Nora!" I couldn't believe it. The bright silver hook had buried itself with a thump in Alan Jimson's eyebrow and the spoon spun and wobbled at his every move. He looked at Tim and Ned who were trying hard not to laugh. Alan shook his head and the spoon flashed and twisted.

"He's done it again," he said quietly. He turned to me, his face full of disappointment. "Me dad'll have to cut it out with plyers. He'll kill me." He took the rod away from me, snipped the line a bit above the lure, and reeled in.

"You've done it again," he said. Then he shrugged and walked away.

Under the Blue Sky

Having experienced everything the cosmos had to offer, for it was the fifth week of the summer holidays and we boys had exhausted everything within our ken, we wandered aimlessly around the outskirts of the village, hoping that something would turn up. My mother had banned us from the house. She knew only too well the effects of having bored children underfoot.

"I blame the teachers," she would say, "Six weeks holiday they help themselves to and us lumbered with flamin' kids! No wonder they grow into hooligans."

As we were wondering what we could do to brighten our day and release us from the doldrums of boredom, salvation arrived in an odd though familiar form. Down Black Road there approached the laughable outline of one of our school friends. His clothes were the usual hand-me-downs, though his being one of twelve meant that they had had further to go, and his knees were, well, filthy. The tidemark around his neck was stark and worthy at least of a hastily washed miner, yet it could not be said that it looked out of place as it matched his haircut admirably. This his father had imposed to save the sixpence charged by the barber. One could tell.

Blessed (if that word suits) with so many faults from which to choose a nickname for this lad, you may be surprised to learn that none of the aforementioned made the grade: there was one more thing about him from whence his handle sprang. Betwixt red nose and thin lips he was constantly accompanied by a glazed discharge, which, as I recall, never dried up. We called him Snot.

Trundling by his side was the remains of a bicycle older than our combined ages. The tyres showed in more than one place glimpses of naked inner tube and the brakes were non-existent.

"It's got no brakes," said Ned.

"It's got a reflector!" countered Snot, eyes wide as he pointed to the back of the saddle. That was impressive. Bikes of such antiquity rarely had the 'extras' and although it no longer possessed a mudguard upon which to mount it, the reflector had been nonetheless salvaged and Snot thought it sufficiently impressive to counterbalance the absence of any brakes.

"The lamp's tied on with string!" cried Jack in disbelief.

"So?" said Snot with sudden scorn, "It doesn't work anyway." His eyes rolled as if to express dismay at such a stupid assumption on Jack's behalf. Nobody could expect it to work if it was tied on with string. The machine, as was usual with homemade bikes, had a fixed wheel, which meant that the pedals rotated constantly whilst it was in motion, both forwards and backwards. The advantage of this was obvious (said Snot) and was demonstrated with great dexterity as he rode backwards in ever decreasing circles until at last he fell off in a dizzy stupor. Of course everyone else had to have a go and with varying degrees of success (none in my case) we all tried out the bike. Howls of laughter accompanied each tumble and as we examined our cuts and scrapes the 'plan' was announced.

"I've got an idea," said Jack. "Let's ride it down Grange Bank!" Grange Bank is a ribbon of tarmac that connects the road at the top of the valley with the one at the bottom. It takes a direct route to the halfway point then turns abruptly to the right; a corner of ninety degrees. A chorus of affirmation erupted, though—cowardly me—I was praying that someone else would be selected to be the heroic rider. Of course it had to be Snot. Goodness knows why any sane person would want to ride a bike with no brakes down a one-in-four hill but, true to form, he volunteered. So we pumped him full of bull; visions of glory and all that, then we set off along the New Road chattering and full of excitement.

It wasn't a hot day but it was pleasantly warm. Despite the sun being veiled every now then in a thin covering of grey, it was mostly sunny and we knew it wouldn't rain as we made fair progress toward the bank some miles distant. Jack barked out orders to hurry along whenever we dawdled—which was often as the wild strawberries were beginning to ripen and naturally drew our attention to the railway embankment where they grew. Jack wouldn't tolerate this, partly because it delayed us and partly because he didn't care for strawberries. He devised, therefore, another plan to get us to the bank more quickly.

"We take turns to get a croggie," he said. A croggie was the local name for riding two-on-a-bike, usually behind the rider but in this case we were informed, to my horror, the little 'uns were to ride on the handle bars at the same time. Two on a bike was illegal, Jack explained, three should be OK.

"Who goes first?" asked Snot.

"Oldest to youngest!" Tim and I cried.

"Youngest to oldest!" countered Roger and Ned at the same time. As usual the choice was left to Jack. He chose oldest to youngest. Tim's face dropped when he realized that the oldest, Roger in this case, would ride on the saddle but would be accompanied by the oldest young 'un. That was him. Quite naturally Jack had to direct operations and would go last. No amount of complaining or beseeching could save Tim and he was hoisted onto the handle bar without further discussion. He balanced both feet on top of the stirrup-shaped contraption that had once held the brake blocks. His white-knuckled hands wrapped around the bar and became immovable. Roger deftly cocked his leg over the saddle and Snot, riding in the middle, shifted his weight onto the starboard pedal and with a push from the rest of us they were off.

They gathered speed and hurtled off towards the bridge. The bike wobbled like hell and Roger's legs stuck out like clock hands at twenty past eight. Every few yards Snot's head would rise above all else briefly exposing the back of his haircut before slowly sinking back and out of sight. Of Tim we could see nothing but we certainly knew he was there as he was howling like a banshee. The rest of us were in stitches as we ran along some short distance behind the bike hooting and howling between the laughs.

Now the bridge, which crosses the river directly beneath the railway viaduct, is narrow; that is it can handle only single file traffic. Nonetheless it must be at least twelve feet wide so could easily accommodate four or even five bicycles abreast. But they didn't make it. Snot somehow managed to steer it into the left hand end of the steel bridge and they came to an abrupt halt. As Tim slid across the retaining nut in the middle of the handle bar and Snot came down heavily upon the crossbar, Roger shot forward off the saddle all three let out a surprised 'Oooh!' Despite our mirth, we rushed over and hauled them from the wreckage.

"I hope you didn't bust anything," said Jack.

"I think I'm all right," replied Tim as he brushed himself off.

"Not you, berk! The bike," snorted Jack as he gave it the once over.

"Charming," mumbled Tim. The tumble had not done any apparent harm to the bike or the boys so we carried on, to my relief, via Shank's pony not stopping until we reached Snowdon's farm a half-mile short of Grange Bank. Just there an ash tree grew in the corner of a clover field and such was its structure that even I could climb it. Year after year starlings nested in a fork halfway up; year after year we would climb up and take a peek. The birds were long gone by this time of the season but we couldn't pass up an opportunity to reaffirm our dislike of them by sniffing their vacated nest site. They were for this very reason colloquially known as 'stinkers.'

"Cor! What a pong!" somebody said, though to be honest I don't think it did, yet we all agreed and pegged our noses.

"Gerrouta that bloody field!" bellowed a harsh voice. Across the field approached a purple-faced and obviously annoyed farmer, his size elevens covering two yards at a stride.

"It's the gadgee!" went up the frantic cry. It was indeed the gadgee and we were down the tree, across the field and over the fence in no time flat. In rescuing the bike, Snot had to suffer some well-placed boots-up-the-arse for his trouble. Finally he scrambled away from the wrath of the irate farmer. When he finally caught us up (we had run off and left him, of course), we stood at the bottom of Grange Bank staring towards the top. It seemed an awful long way and it occurred to us at the same moment that it was time to boost Snot's ego a little if he was to perform. He was, however, preoccupied; mumbling something about one day getting even with 'that scabby farmer sod' and as he said aloud "I'll get that get!" Roger seized upon his words and said:

" Yeah, you show him what you dare do! You show him!" That was all it needed. Once again the young bravado gazed around at us (and also, I think, at some immense invisible audience) then, pushing the bike before him, cried, 'Let's go!' and we all cheered like mad. Just as we neared the summit Ned noticed an old car tyre wedged in the fence to one side of the road and, with a little help from Tim and myself, he pulled it free and began to roll it up the hill intending, of course, to bowl it back down. It was quite a small tyre, liberally covered in bits of leaf-litter, cobwebs and red-bummed spiders, but that didn't deter Ned in the least. Five minutes later six boys, a bike and an old car tyre were silhouetted under the blue sky against the billowing clouds. We were all smiles.

"Right then," said Jack turning to the rider after a few moments of hard panting.

"Right then," replied Snot. You'd think he'd be scared or something but he wasn't. We slapped his back and shook his hand. I pretended I had a trumpet and gave him a fanfare that seemed to do no harm. He veritably leapt aboard the bike and with neither wave nor adieu whizzed off down that long, steep hill. Ned gave the tyre a shove and it wobbled off in the same direction. We stared wide-eyed at our hero as he zoomed toward the junction half way down. Small tatters of clothing, picked up in the slipstream that whipped around Snot's speedy form, vibrated aloud. He never even saw the hedge loom before him. We could do nought but gaze horrified as the bike deviated neither left nor right. He didn't even seem to make an effort to negotiate the corner. I winced as he hit the fence. Surely he was thrown? But no! The bike smashed through the fence and left a gap three feet wide. Whole branches of hawthorn were entangled in the frame and impaled upon Snot but, by the lord Harry, he held on!

We reached the fence and peered over it just in time to see the bike (and, sadly, its rider) finally succumb to the vibrations caused by the bumpy nature of the pasture. The front wheel and the forks parted company and the gallant jockey was flung unceremoniously to the ground, though he travelled some distance on his stomach before coming to rest with his chest inches away from a newly deposited cow-pat. He, and we, heaved a sigh of relief and paused for a few moments to thank the stars that nothing more serious had befallen the brave Snot.

Just then, from the corner of my eye, I perceived the black and wraith-like image of the tyre as it silently slid past and, by a million-to-one chance, zipped through the very gap in the hedge made moments before by the entry of the bike. We watched in disbelief as it skipped over the divots toward the unaware and prostrate shape in the grass. Reprieve almost came at the last moment as the tyre hit

Snot's bum and became airborne—but no! It clipped him smartly on the back of the head and pushed his entire face into the cowpat.

He never did believe we didn't do it on purpose.

The Fly

I remember the day Mrs. Beaker decided for certain that her family was moving to Newton Aycliffe. It stands out like those other childhood events of enormous importance that scraped a groove in my memory deep and wide: the day Ned's chicken finally laid an egg; starting school; my first encounter with the dentist; the time Christine Ford kissed me right on the mouth.

It was summertime and my brothers had given me the early-morning slip when I was still half asleep. It turned out that they'd gone off hunting water rats, a skill requiring concentration and stealth—attributes they felt I lacked in abundance. When I discovered they were missing, I went scuffling around the village looking for something to do. I bumped into Billy Beaker at the top of Low King Street.

"Hello," he said, cowering as he checked around for my brothers. They couldn't stick Beaker and they often boxed his lugs and tweaked his nose. They thought it was very funny and I must admit I laughed at him tons. "Will you play with me today?"

"Play what?" I asked. Beaker leaned back and stared at the sky as if he were searching for inspiration. I was hoping he'd invite me into his house because as an only child he had some incredibly nifty stuff to play with. He was the only kid I knew that got a *pair* of six-shooters for his birthday. The rest of us got only one, and often as not that had belonged to an older brother at some time. Hand-me-downs were common and mostly it was an honour to inherit the pre-owned objects that had passed the test of time with a brother. Bikes, in particular, were bought for the eldest and handed down to junior siblings—painted and repainted until they were worn out. Beaker got his first bike brand new when he was only five and it was replaced with a bigger new one just two years later. That's why some kids didn't like him.

"Let's play in your house," I said.

Beaker's suddenly looked uncomfortable. He shifted from one foot to the other and pulled at the corner of his cardigan sweater.

"Could we not stay outside?" he pleaded. "Only my mother is in a bit of a mood." I had heard Beaker's dad use that expression before, and I must admit I was a bit curious as to what it meant.

"We can ask your dad if we can play inside," I suggested.

"He's not home. Anyway, he does what Mam says."

I had once overheard a woman in the fish-and-chip shop say that Mr. Beaker was a broken man. He had a hangdog look about him and never seemed very happy. He was one of the few men in the village who had never been out of work, on account of Mrs. Beaker's father got him a membership in some kind of freemason's guild, but, according to the chip-shop expert, none of the other men would switch places with him for all the coal in Newcastle.

"How come your mam doesn't like your dad?"

"Cos he's good for nothing."

"Who sez?"

"She does. Every night almost. She gets mad at people who sit around and do nothing. I stop out of her way when she gets in one of her moods."

"Doesn't your dad help out?"

"He says there's nothing to do. She cleans up about twice a day and we're not allowed to mess anything up."

Beaker's dad was a bit of a mystery. He had an accent and my mam told me he 'wasn't from around here.' Apparently Mrs. Beaker had married him hoping to go and live wherever it was he was from, but for whatever reason they never went. I thought it must be because he didn't want his friends to meet her as she was always shouting at him. And Billy. And me. But she was very clean and tidy. Almost a sickness I thought.

"If we don't play inside, we don't play at all," I said in a cold sort of way. I have no idea what I would have come back with if he'd said O.K. but, as it was, he was desperate for a playmate and agreed to go inside under the strict understanding that we didn't make a mess and we scarpered the moment we heard Mrs. Beaker raise her voice.

We duly entered the house through the back kitchen door. Beaker's house had once been a cobbler's shop and the back door was one of the kind that the top half could be opened while the bottom remained shut, or vice versa. It was excellent both for climbing over and limbo dancing under, depending on which half was shut, of course. We did each activity several times.

Mrs. Beaker liked to have the doors open through the day and that meant she got a great number of flies around the place. My favourites were greenbottles because of their metallic sheen and relative rareness. Next I like bluebottles because of their mad flight patterns — I had never been able to catch one except against a window. Houseflies, the most common at Beaker's house, were boring little things that flew in uninteresting, angular circles in the middle of the kitchen.

Mrs. Beaker disliked all flies, all bugs and most children. She especially encouraged Billy to stay away from me as I caused trouble. Her words—quite unfair I thought, as I only played with Beaker as a last resort to prevent death by boredom. Hanging from the light fixture in the middle of their back kitchen was a spiral tape of flypaper. It looked a bit like an enormous butterfly tongue covered in currants, except they weren't currants they were dead and dying flies. Eventually, every fly that strayed into Beaker's house succumbed to the lure of whatever was pasted to the surface of the fly strip. They landed, stuck fast and expired.

"What shall we play?" asked Beaker. "We have to stay quiet or we'll get in trouble with my mother."

"Let's play with your cowboy stuff," I suggested.

"We can't," said Beaker. "It's in my bedroom and I daren't go up or my mother will clip my ear for being inside."

I pondered the situation for a minute. It was incredible to me that Beaker had his own room. I felt both sorry for him in his loneliness and jealous at the same time because I had shared a room with Ned and Tim since the beginning of time. I was also wondering how his mother could be so bad as to prevent us getting at all of Beaker's playthings—a collection that was widely understood among the kids in the village to be bigger than Doggart's toy department.

"Well, what can we play with?" I demanded. Beaker looked around the back kitchen, frantic to find something to keep me amused and in his company. He rummaged through a drawer and held up several unlikely objects, each time looking at my face to see whether or not I approved. Spatulas, corkscrews, icing bags and the accompanying piping nozzles, all manner of culinary aids. Secretly, I liked Beaker. I think it was because when I was with him he took on the role I normally played myself. That is, he went to great lengths to please me and in doing so made a prat of himself.

"Billy," I said. "This stuff's no good. What can we do with it?"

Beaker flailed the air with a ladle.

"Tennis, anyone?" he said.

Around the handle of the ladle was an elastic band. Mrs. Beaker, like almost every other woman in the village, made jam in the autumn and over each jar placed waxed paper held down with an elastic band. In the back of the drawer there was a whole packet of them in every colour imaginable.

"Let's make gats," I said. Gats was what we called catapults, or slingshots if you went to the pictures a lot. You tied several rubber bands end to end and voila! ... a weapon capable of firing a paper pellet at high velocity. I was rather good at firing these things and I had a suspicion that Beaker was not. In which case, of course, I would have nothing to fear when we declared war on each other.

I loosed the first pellet before Beaker had strung together his rubber bands and by the time his gat was ready he had several welts on his face and bare legs. When he finally fought back, his first shot smacked the back of his hand and made him yowl louder than any of my shots did. I deeked behind the kitchen table and fired again. Beaker returned the volley woefully wide of the mark, took another hit and shot himself for a second time.

"Skinchies," he said. That was the word for securing a truce. It was duly honoured while I taught him how to fire the gat without whacking his own hand. I stood behind him and as he held out his hand I took a bead along his arm and moved his other hand so that the pellet would zip between his thumb and forefinger rather than into his palm. We were totally absorbed in this when the temperature of the room seemed to drop a degree or two.

Mrs. Beaker had come quietly down the stairs, drawn toward the sounds of mirth. She filled the doorway and blocked much of the light from the back kitchen as she stepped into the room. She wasn't a big woman, quite trim, actually, but she had enormous presence and piercing eyes. When she looked at me I got this guilty expression whether or not I'd been up to no good. She was convinced I was some kind of jinx and she would not be shaken from that belief. I felt it was unfair. Yes, whenever I was with Billy we got into scrapes, but I was the only kid in the village willing to play with him so I felt I deserved some credit. I mean…all kids get into trouble, don't they?

"What are you up to?" she said in a sharp whisper that slit the air. Billy just about passed out. I had drawn back the gat fully by then. In a panic Beaker discharged the pellet, which hit a colander, ricocheted vertically and cut the thread that held up the fly strip. The coil of shiny paper dropped like a spotted snake and wrapped around Mrs. Beaker's head and face. Without thinking she filled her lungs to shout at us and in doing so let the paper slip into her mouth. She froze. A not-quite-dead housefly rattled its wings next to her eye.

Bzzt...bzzt

Before the full horror of what had happened dawned I looked once at Billy and knew it was time to run. I can only imagine that Beaker's mother caught him before he'd either deeked under the half door or climbed over it. I only know I pulled it shut behind me when I took off. Somehow Billy Beaker never managed a clean escape.

The Harvest

August. It was the time of year that I love the best. Frosted sunshine plated the hedgerows and jewelled them with argentine spider webs. Finches gorged themselves on hawthorn berries, and, early in the mornings, I could blow pretend smoke from pretend cigarettes in full view of passing adults.

I had been chucked out of the house—get out an' play, yer dad's just come off the night shift—earlier than usual, and as I stalked the garden allotment I was surprised by Nutty Wicker's soft voice.

"Hello, Philip. On your own, are you?"

"Yes, Nutty, I mean... Mr. Wicker."

"That's all right, son. Did you think I don't know my own nickname? I've been called a lot worse than that." You couldn't phase Nutty. He was cool as cress. Once, when he woke up to find a whole row of carrots had been stolen from his garden, he simply nodded his head.

"I expect this poor chap has more mouths to feed than I do." I always felt good in his company. He had the kind of face that makes you think its owner is on the verge of laughter. Consequently, I giggled even more than usual when I was near him.

"It's gonna be a good day," he said, looking me right in the eye. "Harvest begins today."

"Oh, yes?" I said, "I wish I could go haymaking, but my brothers say I'm too small. Farmer Stivvy sez I'm not big enough to see over a bale, let alone lift one."

"Never mind," Nutty replied, "You shall help me in Mrs. Stivvy's orchard." He wore his wizard smile again, and I was certain that he was going to say something I'd like. I was right.

"The berries are ripe—brambles, bilberries, goosegogs—it's jam-time, Philip!" He could not have made me happier if he'd slipped me a shilling.

"Tell yer mam you're coming with me an' not to bother with bait or nowt. There'll be plenty to eat at the farm." Bait, in this case, meant packed lunch. "Look sharp, now. We'll need to be there by eight o' clock." I took off without another word.

It wasn't thirty minutes since I'd filled up on toast and Marmite, but already I was salivating at the prospect of Mrs. Stivvy's farm fare. My brothers were donning jerkins and pullovers as I burst in.

"Mam, I'm going to Stivvy's."

The boys looked at me in unison.

"Oh, no you're not, " said Jack, "Mr. Stivvy said you're too small. And you lark about too much, and..."

"I'm going with Nutty."

"Mr. Wicker," corrected my mother, "All right." I waited just long enough to enjoy the gape-a-rama from my brothers, then sped back through the door, back up Black Road and over the fields to Nutty's stone cottage.

The front of the house was covered in greenery—climbing, vine-like plants of which Nutty was very fond. He collected these native evergreens from the surrounding countryside and trained them up trellises cut from alder. Over the doorway hung a sign knifed from a holly burl. Holme House it said, and a wee wooden mouse ran down one side. Around the back was a pile of thin willow wands that Nutty used for basket making. His basketwork had provided a source of income for him in the past, but with the advent of polythene carrier-bags he couldn't give his wares away. After all, who wanted wood when you could have plastic?

He was sitting on a carpenter's horse talking to a small piece of timber when I found him.

"In here," he said, "Is the shape of a saw handle. All I have to do is cut away the excess." He was smiling, so I knew he was pulling my leg. Nutty never pulled anyone's leg without giving an enormous clue that it was being done.

"All ready, young fella?"

"All ready."

"Got your spoovy-jigglers?"

"Eh?"

"Right then, by the left...quick...quack!" And off he went, skipping a dozen steps, marking time until I caught up, and quacking like a maniacal mallard in the morning sun. When I asked my dad how old Nutty was he told me he'd been around since Adam was a lad. Father McShame said 'You'd think he was twelve,' but Nutty told me outright - I'm as old as my tongue and a little bit older than my teeth.

When we got as far as the river, we stopped to look at a tree. It looked like all the others to me; I named trees by process of elimination. No acorns - not oak. No conkers - not horse chestnut. No hips - not rose.

"Know what this is?"

"It's not an elderberry." I said. He gave me a queer look.

"Very good. But what is it?"

"I dunno." He was delighted.

"It's a hazel! All those green things are nuts. We'll pick 'em next month and they'll be ready for the year's end." He jumped up at the lower branches and pulled down a handful of greenery that included several furry, unripe cobnuts.

"I know every hazel for miles around," he said, "That's why they call me Nutty!" That's one reason, I thought.

Back on the deeply rutted cart track, we continued our walk as dew dried and the sun rose higher in the blue sky. I asked a question-a-minute, all of which were answered. Of course, I couldn't tell when the answer was wrong, or opinionated, or what. It was all gospel to me. For years after, I believed that aphids came from cuckoo spit. I must have had my eyes elsewhere as he smiled and spun that one.

Stivvy's farm was picture book set on a floodplain in the bottom of the valley. Wheat fields quilted the surrounding land and potato plants nearer the farmhouse made the homestead a green oasis. Dogs barked as we approached.

"Twenty minutes early," said Nutty, looking at the sky. The sun was his watch, and, as he said, it never stopped and it was never wrong. "Time for a drink of milk before we start." We crossed the barnyard, carefully avoiding the morning's cowpats, and went into the dairy. The cows were back out in the river meadow by this time, but their milk was running across washboard coolers into churns, ready for collection. In one stall, next door in the byre, Mr. Stivvy was hand milking a big black-and-white Friesian that would not submit to the machine.

"The lad wants a drop of milk, Farmer."

"Well, then. He'd better come and get it."

It was all a bit convenient, and I should have guessed they were razzing me. The farmer stood up and I took his place on the cracket behind the cow. The first thing she did was lash me in the face with a muck-encrusted tail.

"Gordon Bennett," I said, somewhat surprised.

"It's just grass," said Nutty, "Beast eat only grass, and that won't hurt you."

Hurt no. Stink yes. It was all I could do not to throw up. Mr. Stivvy held the tail to one side, and both he and Nutty wore broad grins.

"Put yer hands between her legs an' grab her titties," said the farmer. I followed the instruction and took hold of the two teats at the rear. They weren't a bit as I'd expected—what thought, if any, I'd given them led me to expect something like a rubber glove filled with water. But they were quite meaty, really. I can't say I was keen. Of course nothing came out of them. I squished and pulled just as I'd seen the farmer do, but ne'er a drop did that cow pass.

"I think it mus' be empty."

"Look out. Let's have a look-see," said Stivvy, dropping the tail and helping me to one side. To my relief, he couldn't get milk either.

"Well, I'm jiggered," he said, removing his flat cap and scratching his thin, silvery hair. "What do you reckon, Mr. Wicker? Any ideas?" Nutty's prowess with natural lore was well known. I had no doubt that he could correct the problem. He leaned in and looked at the huge, veined udder. Then he leaned against the cow and listened.

"There it is," he said, "Engine's stopped." Mr. Stivvy pressed his ear to the animal and confirmed it.

"Have a listen," he said to me, "What do you hear?"

"Nowt."

"Exactly."

"Sit back down, Farmer," said Nutty, "We'll pump it by hand." Nutty took the cow's tail and began to manipulate it up and down, like a standpipe handle. Mr. Stivvy began his rhythmic caress of the teats. On the third stroke the milk returned and my estimation of Nutty, if such a thing was possible, rose even higher, and my jaw dropped open in surprise. The price for gaping in a milking shed is a bluebottle in the mouth, and while I was paying it I noticed Nutty and the farmer laughing through clenched teeth. Well, I suppose a fly in the mouth is funny, right?

Finally, I was offered milk from a ladle dipped in a churn. It was silky and still tasted like it came from an animal rather than something squeezed from roots.

"Dad sez you can get T.B. from new milk," I said. I had actually known kids in the village who had died from it, but I didn't know exactly what it was. Who did? Mr. Stivvy waved the ladle back and forth in front of my face.

"Past-yer-eyes. Now it's all right," he said, and the two of them fell to laughing again. The farmer yelled *cush* and *gertcha*, and the cow left the byre and skipped off back to its sisters, followed by the chuckling farmer.

"Time for work," said Nutty, and we walked to the back of the farmhouse where Mrs. Stivvy's berry bushes were neatly regimented in the sun. She was a wiry woman with steel-grey hair and a ruddy face. Her arms were brown and sinewy and her eyes were almost black. When she smiled, which was almost as often as Nutty, they just about disappeared among the rays of laugh lines. Just about the only thing that I didn't like about her was her merciless habit of pinching your face.

"Hello, young man," she said, tweaking my cheek far harder than one would normally expect even as punishment. I let out an involuntary 'ayah!' and she gritted her teeth and pinched the other side.

"Such a face," she said, "Oh, I could eat you, tell yer mam!" Now my face was an acceptable shade of red and I looked like the rest of the yokels.

"He's come to help me with the picking," said Nutty. That excited her again and, before the pain from the first attack had subsided, she pinched both sides of my face and concertina'd my cheeks till it sounded like the sloshing of hair tonic.

"Argh..." I managed. What a bittersweet woman she was. Nutty was more than fond of her and he didn't care who knew.

"How about a cuddle before we start?"

"Get away with you," she said, flicking a tea towel at his behind. "The baskets are by the back door." Nutty bowed gracefully, turned and gave me a wink, and veritably leapt through the open door.

I liked the way Nutty worked. He was industrious without toiling. Frequent breaks, always caused by something he discovered—a bug, a stone, a passing bird—and simply had to tell me about. Between these breaks he sang and hummed and chatted about everything and anything.

"Where were you born?" I asked.

"Right here. Well, in my cottage."

"Is the cottage very old?"

"Older than the village by a long chalk. My father and his father were born there. Back as far as can be. Same stones as the Saxon church in Escomb. Same stones as the circles on Frosterley Common. Romans knew Holme House. Britons, even pechs." He pronounced this word like the Scottish loch.

"What's a pech?" I mimicked.

Nutty rolled a gooseberry around his mouth and spat out a piece of stem.

"What do they learn you at school?" he said. "Pechs were the first ones to come to these islands. Long before the tall white people. They were sawn-off little buggers with brown skin. They had wonderful powers of healing."

"Where'd they go?"

"Chased out. People were scared of the little folk, the brownies. They didn't have anything to do with each other, and the pechs disappeared into faerie and folk tales," I looked at Nutty for the tell-tale smile, but his face was serious and almost sad. "How you doing with the goosegogs?" I was doing about one-tenth the rate he was.

"You have to learn to pick and listen at the same time. Can't stop for nattering."

"Faeries aren't real though. They're made up aren't they?" I said, upping my picking somewhat. Nutty tossed a berry house-high and caught it in his mouth. It was a particularly sour one and made him shut one eye as he swallowed.

Ooooh...good 'un!

"Make believe, eh? Well, young fella, it's seems a bit much of a coincidence that they are part of so much folklore. The Irish called them leprechauns, the Scots called 'em pechs, up here we call them brownies. Germans stories call them dwarfs. Elves, pixies, duergars, boggarts—it's just too much to ignore. I'm sure Shakespeare never intended the faerie-folk to wear little wings and carry magic wands as we see them in Midsummer Night's Dream. I'm sure he knew them as the queer-faced little humans they were."

"Who's Shakespeare?" I asked.

"Crikey! Pick some berries will you?"

Over the fields behind the harvester, my brothers were stripped to the waist and sweating. When the bales of hay fell from the back of the combine, their job was to stand them on end leaned one against the other. Farmer Stivvy still called these structures 'sheaves' though the grains were stored in silos miles away at the wheat-pool. Every now and then I looked across the stubbled fields and waved at the older boys, but they never saw me. I wished I could be with them as I knew they'd be having great fun. But I was content to be with Nutty, hearing about the countryside that was like a sea surrounding the industrial island of the village.

Sometime around noon we stopped for what Nutty called 'a bite' and what I called a feast. Mrs. Stivvy served up piping hot tea in enormous pint mugs banded in blue. All the boys, and Nutty and Mr. Stivvy, sat at an outside table while the farmer's wife performed her miracles. Doorsteps of farmhouse bread, crusty and warm from the oven, were laid in mountainous piles in the middle of the table. We helped ourselves to these and lashed them generously with new butter and the strawberry jam made earlier in the year. Apples, berries and crumbly white cheese were there for those that wished. After half an hour we had eaten more that we normally did in a whole day.

"How's the berries coming?" asked the farmer.

"Great," I told him.

"One for the basket, one for me, eh?" he said. How could he have seen so far over the fields? He and Nutty began their esoteric chuckling again and I looked away. Jack and Rodge were showing off their wasp welts. They had unearthed a nest during the course of the morning and had each received several stings in their screaming retreat from that side of the field. Now that they'd stopped hurting, the boys were quite proud of them.

"I got a gooseberry prick in my thumb," I said.

"How would you like a poke in the eye?" Big kids have a way of putting minor injuries into just the right perspective. Jack estimated there would be another two hours work before the last field was cut and we'd all have to go home.

"When the box is left I get dibs on the beating," he said. Gosh, how I wish I'd listened when mother was teaching us that language.

"What's a box? Who's gonna get a beating?"

"The box is the last part of the wheat to be cut. All the mice an' rabbits hide in it. I go through it and chase them out and...wham!"

"Wham what?"

"You'll see," said Nutty. "Come on, time we got back to those bushes. If we hurry we be done afore the other boys. Let's get cracking."

The gathering broke and we returned to our respective tasks. Mrs. Stivvy brought out a slab of seed cake for her pickers, but I was hard pushed to get any of it down. Nutty ate like a creature preparing to hibernate. Anything that passed by caught his fancy and was scoffed.

"You're too skinny, kid. You should get some meat on your bones before the winter gets here," he advised. "There'll be no fresh fruit then. Only taties and turmits."

"I like taties."

"Just as well."

We gathered the remainder of the gooseberries and went to the bilberry bushes furthest away from the house. These berries stained my hands (and of course, my mouth) but I was surprised to find the juice was blood red and not purple like the fruit itself. After half an hour these were stripped and in one of Nutty's wicker baskets ready for the farmer's wife.

"Bilberries make the most wonderful wine," said Nutty, shaking the contents of the containers to make an assessment of the day's labour. "I like a glass at winter solstice to remind me that she's coming back."

"Who's that, then?"

"The earth mother," he said in a disappointed sort of voice. "You like to be here in the fields don't you, Philip?"

"Oh, yeah. It's great."

"Yes. When is your family moving to the new town?"

I hadn't thought about that in days. Not since the bulldozers had rolled through Vulcan Terrace and cleared away the ugly blue-brick cottages at the lower point of the village. We lived at the opposite end and, despite mother's specific instructions to the contrary, had gone to watch the workmen do their stuff. All the kids cheered when the walls caved in amid clouds of dust, and pennies could be earned from old men who bargained with the demolition crew.

"How much for this? How much? You're a bloody thief! Here, son. Carry this up to my house an' I'll give yer a penny."

We joyfully took the coppers for what seemed to me to be the most useless pieces of junk imaginable: pipes, sinks, closets that had been screwed to the wall and now had an open side.

"Are you still here?" asked Nutty.

"Oh, yes. I was just thinking. I wonder if we'll get streets in the same order as here." I looked at Nutty and he wore the exact same expression that dad had on his face when he told me where my dog was the day after she killed Kit Carson's chickens.

"My guess is that you won't have to worry about all these old fogies when you go to the new place. Most of them will move in with relatives in the other villages. The new town is too expensive for them. Your dad has a good job with the railway! You'll be living in luxury."

That cheered me up. I didn't really like some of the people who used to live in Vulcan Terrace. They were always pinching coal from the railway embankment and their yards were strewn with bits of old cars and motorbikes, though none of them owned one.

"Where are you going?" I said.

"Bless my bunions," replied Nutty. "I'm not going nowhere. My cottage is outside the shadow of rural planning. It's on a ley between the stone circles and St. Wilf's hill. Couldn't get any safer." He

71

explained to me about the connecting lines that ran imaginary paths across the land. I could not quite grasp who'd made them or why, but he seemed confident that they were there. Everything along them was sort of sacred, he told me. But the village had been built on top of the ley and not under its protection.

"Eventually, all things must pass. But the connection never breaks. I got it from a friend of my father. My old dad never had it himself. It don't necessarily run in families, although it tends to do so more with women."

"What are you talking about?"

"About you! She likes you, does the earth mother. And if she takes a shine to you, no matter where you live—city, town, or country—you'll become connected, like it or not. What do yer think about that?"

"I ate too many goosegogs."

The time arrived for the straw-box to be emptied and we walked over the field to where the boys and Farmer Stivvy stood with sticks and shovels by the edges of the wheat square. The harvester stood to one side, still running but idling. It had cut the lanes of grain in inevitable circles until all that was left was this island in a corn-yellow sea. Jack strode into the stand and beat the stalks with his stick, shouting and whooping as he went.

Run, rabbit, run, rabbit, run ,run, run...

Here comes the farmer with his gun, gun, gun...

Suddenly, dozens of field mice poured from the safety of the last stand. Six rabbits, a hare, and even a waddling hedgehog made the break for freedom and a new life in some other field. But they had tarried too long, and the village boys were upon them with the instruments of death. Nothing escaped, and after the screams of delight from the boys died down, the spoils were divided up so that each got something for the pot. Stivvy handed me a rabbit with its head stoved in.

"I don't want it."

"Yes, you do," said Nutty. "It will make a good dinner for the family. You won't forget this will you?"

"Not likely." And as we walked home I couldn't shake the idea that the rabbit, and not the berries, had stained my hands that day. Surely it heard the ominous approach of the harvester. Why had it not left that stand while there was still time?

Beaker Goes West

It was potato-picking time and Rodge, Ned and Tim had managed to sneak off while my back was turned. They'd gone to East Moor where they had been told they were shoo-ins for the first three hirings. The local potato baron, Tubby Murphy, was a friend of my dad's and he'd had a word on their behalf. Potato picking paid the colossal sum of fifteen-bob-a-day, and with a bit of luck you'd only have to cough over half of it towards housekeeping.

"It builds character," my dad always said as he separated his sons from the root of all evil.

"You'll only spend it on rubbish," my mother always said. The truth was, of course, that being able to contribute to the family budget was a reward greater than the money itself. I didn't care because I never got a job. I told myself it was better not to lower myself to stand in the knot of hopefuls who hired themselves out to grub around in mud and worms for ten hours or more. Also, of course, because my mother wouldn't let me go anyway. I sat on the front step for a while with my dad and we drank tea from enormous white pint-pots banded in blue. Mine was only half filled because I couldn't lift a full one.

"On a rainy day, some of the spuds weigh more than this mug," my dad said. "Anyway, this is better than plodging around in clarts, isn't it?"

"Yes," I said. But secretly I looked forward to the day when I would go spud-bashing with the older boys and earn my first wage. In the meantime, I had my own plans. Later that day Beaker and his family were scheduled to leave the village forever and head for a new life in the Newton Aycliffe. I would casually call by and see if he wanted to come out and play just so I could get a shufty at what was going on.

"More tea?" said Dad.

"Another time, perhaps." And I left my astonished father on the doorstep and went back inside to get my muffler and balaclava helmet.

The sky was pewter-dull and the street was wet from the light but steady rain. Little rivers ran through the stones and converged in fast-flowing streams at the sides of the unpaved road. I screwed up a toffee wrapper I found in the bottom of a pocket and threw it into stream in the worn gutter outside our house. Then I ran alongside it toward the bottom of the street. At the drain the paper boat disappeared, but by then I was opposite Beaker's house—just where I wanted to be. The curtains were gone and newspapers were spread across all the windows. I wondered why people always hung newspapers upside down when it seemed obvious that it made them difficult for passers by to read.

Out on the road Beaker's dad and a man in what had once been white overalls were loading a big van. They seemed to know just what they were doing and never hit any of the furniture off the walls or the doorjamb. I was wondering how to convince Beaker's dad to let him come out and play for a few minutes when I heard Mrs. Beaker raise her voice in frustration.

"Billy. Get the hell out from under my feet." Then there was the familiar smack of bare hand on bare ear and one yelp later Beaker was standing next to me out on the road.

"Now, kid."

"Now, Philip. We're shifting."

"I know. Want to make a dam in the gutter?" And of course he said yes. What sane kid wouldn't? We kicked stones from the road over to the drain and stuffed the cracks with dead leaves and the ample litter of gum wrappers, ice-cream wrappers and fish-and-chips paper that was blown into the corner of the street on a regular basis.

"Shall you come and see me at the new house?" asked Beaker. I instinctively looked around. My brothers and the older kids couldn't stand Beaker because he was a bit of a girl's blouse and ran to tell Mrs. Trout tales a lot at school. But as that wasn't too different from my own style I kind of felt an affinity with him. Still, it wasn't good form to be caught being too pally with him, so I had got into the habit of checking behind me when I was with him.

"Mebbe."

"When is your family moving?"

"Dad says we'll move over his dead body."

"That's what my dad said too."

"Where are you movin' to?"

"Aycliffe. It's got everything. Library. Pictures. Supermarket. A park with swings and a slide."

"What's a supermarket?"

"Dunno. But Mam's keen on it and Dad's not. I heard them arguing." And if arguments in Beaker's house went anything like those in my own, his mother would win out.

Under the thin drizzle we hunted around for clemmies. Clemmies are stones that are sized between pebbles and rocks. Any weight, any shape. Beaker was good at finding flat ones that are exactly what you need when you're building a gutter dam. These days, when entertainment is almost totally dependent on plastic things that require batteries, the art of gutter damming is about lost.

To succeed, you need to lug the two biggest clemmies you can find into the gutter and sit them side by side. In front of these, before the water gets too deep, you place old newspapers. These get sodden very quickly and plug the gap between the two stones so you have to be nifty with the next stage, which is placing smaller clemmies immediately upstream from the newspaper. The penultimate step is to tear up any remaining newspaper or other debris of a wettable type, and scatter it some way upstream so that by the time it reaches the dam it is waterlogged and plugs up any small holes that remain.

When Beaker and I got to this stage, I dropped a few pebbles into the dam pool and effectively sealed the bottom off. At this point a flood extending around the sides of the dam prompted the serious business of beavering more and more clemmies to arrest the rising waters. It's futile, of course, but I hoped with luck the dam would hold until an impressive pond lapped at both sides of the road.

"Not bad eh?" Beaker and I stood to the side and looked on with grins that would not have been bigger if we had just built the Aswan dam on the Nile.

"I'm nithered," I said as the wind stole through my wet clothes and made me shiver. "Let's get some tea at my house."

"I'll have to ask my mother," said Beaker, wearing a sudden look of dread.

"She chucked you out didn't she?" I asked.

"Oh, yes," said Beaker, brightening. "Let's go." How could we possibly have known that the furniture moving was at that very moment coming to completion and that the family would be delayed by exactly the same amount of time as Beaker spent at my house?

My mother was exceedingly nice to Beaker I always felt. She was constantly telling me what a good boy he was, and of course it made me sick. But that day I too felt a bit sorry for Beaker. He was to be one of the first to go to the new town and at that point I looked on him as a bit of a Columbus as the journey seemed no safer than looking for a new route to India by sailing west.

"All ready for the off?" my mother said as she placed two pots of steaming tea down on the table next to a plate holding two scones. Beaker was distracted only a moment, but it gave me the time I needed to grab the larger of the scones. Mam sussed the move immediately.

"Now I'm sure that Billy would have taken the smaller one if he'd had first choice," she said.

"Well? He's got it hasn't he?" I smiled. I had waited a long time to be teed up for that joke. We got stuck into the goodies and as Beaker answered questions my mother and I dodged the crumbs.

"My mam's happy to go," he said. "She sez groceries are half the price at the supermarket." Mother's eyebrows rose.

"Half the price, eh?" she said.

"Yes. And there's thirty-one shops in the town centre," Beaker went on. Mother's eyebrows disappeared under her fringe. That was twenty-one more than in the whole of Witton Park—if you excluded the betting shop.

"What's a supermarket?" I asked.

"And there's three bookies." He made it sound like Las Vegas, and I suspect the look my mother cast over her shoulder was to see if my dad was within earshot of that last remark. He had been known to spend as much as five-bob-a-week on horseracing. No wonder she worried about him.

"And Dad's got a job at the plastics factory," Beaker was on a roll. "Twenty-pound-a-week and all the bull you can handle." Bull meant overtime, but it was an expression with which Beaker should not have been familiar so it proved the statement was made verbatim. Twenty pounds a week was unheard of for labourers. I looked at my mother and watched the changes in her expression as she succumbed to the temptations of Newton Aycliffe. And right then I knew we'd be moving after all. Despite the upheaval and all the chaos it would cause. Despite my father's crusade.

"On twenty-pound-a-week a man could buy his wife an automatic washing machine," said Mam. And as she got that far away look in her eyes Beaker and I finished our tea and went back outside.

A crowd of nebbie-noses had gathered to watch the exodus of Beaker's family. Crones in headscarves had been in place in time to scrutinize the last bits of furniture as the men carried them to the van. Mrs. Beaker was livid. When her son and I got to the house she exploded.

"Billy ya bugger! Where've you been? Get in the van this minute. Move." And Beaker was snatched away before I had time to say so long or anything. The pond behind our dam had flooded the road and Mrs. Beaker had to stand right next to the house so she wouldn't get her feet soaked.

"This flood's your doing, isn't it?" she said to me. "I've a good mind to box yer lugs." But I was safe on the opposite side of the lake. She was dressed like she was going either to a dance or to the doctor. Her outfit was dated but very chic. She looked like a wartime movie star with her pencil skirt and short jacket, and she'd had her hair done very nineteen-fifties. She hauled herself up to her full height, made some adjustments to her belt, and called to her husband to back the van up so she could climb in without getting wet. Wordlessly he ground the gears into reverse and stepped on the pedal. The van lurched backward into the pond and a sheet of water whooshed vertically from beneath the back wheels and made straight for Beaker's mam.

In the moment when the wall of water hung in the air like a stoat before a rabbit, Mrs. Beaker's face showed a number of split second changes ranging from initial disbelief through anger and finally to a sort of resignation to the impending disaster. When the flood hit her it was unmerciful in its extent. Her beehive hair-do hung limp at the side of her head and her dress clung with embarrassing accuracy. Bits of leaf and grit were splattered uniformly across her face and her beauty spot had moved. Drips fell rapidly from the end of her nose and one of her earrings was missing. Not a pretty sight.

No one said a word. She looked straight at me and I smiled weakly. Then she turned to the gathering.

"Good riddance to bad rubbish," she said calmly. Her husband jumped down and helped her into the van and off they went.

The Gang Goes Gumshoe

Late summer had arrived in full flush; children began to show race, copper skin and fair hair, pearly teeth and shining eyes, laughing, running, free. By the river and around a fire we stood and awaited the potatoes, newly stolen from an adjacent field they lay among the embers baking slowly. New potatoes are not very good for baking but no one seemed to mind that. The insides were nearly always raw and not eaten anyway. Usually these remains were flung back into the tuber patch from whence they came, or else tossed high into the air to plummet into the river with a satisfying plop. Or you could chuck them at the kids that were swimming.

Deep into the afternoon we decided to call it quits and head home to tea and the blackberry pie that had been baked that morning. Everyone wore their swimming trunks on their heads, as was the custom. It looked silly but left one's hands free to do mischief. The trunks were uniformly dark blue, made of close-knit heavy wool. When wet they were capable of absorbing enormous quantities of water at which time they seemed to weigh in the region of fifty pounds. No amount of hoisting could persuade them to stay in place and swimming trips inevitably included sudden and frequent glimpses of bare bum.

My four brothers and I stopped in the middle of the road bridge and spat through our teeth into the current below. High above, the arches of the railway viaduct soared in redbrick splendour.

"I'll bet," said Roger, "That this is the only place in the world where a bridge, a railway an' a river cross in the same place." Quite a thought. Surely such a phenomenon was at least rare, and as we pondered it an urgent motor-horn sent us scurrying to the sides of the bridge.

"Gerroff the bloody road!" bellowed the irate driver. We stuck up two fingers in the time-honoured manner whilst blowing raspberries, our innovative embellishment.

"I wonder who he is?" I said. "He nearly wiped us out!" There were mumblings of agreement and Jack said:

"We should ask Geordie Tanner."

Geordie Tanner was somewhat of a celebrity in those parts. His recall upon car licence plates was infallible. Collecting and noting numbers was his passion. So good was he that people, by way of test, would point out some motor car climbing the bank on the opposite side of the valley, so far away that one could only just discern its colour.

"What's the number on that one, Geordie?" they would ask. Then eyes would widen when he would promptly answer— something along the lines of: "It's Mr. Bell's Ford Prefect, 1952, two doors, blue, licence number 164-3HN. He's probably goin' up to Bitchburn, his sister lives up there." He knew every car for five miles around and could rattle off their numbers at will. He was never wrong.

Aside from this remarkable gift, Geordie was crackers. He was harmless, and almost endearing, but definitely a few bricks short of a load. Little children ran off in terror at his approach, but mothers mothered him, and men and older boys would tease him by asking about some car or other. He did not pay any mind to it, always smiling beguiling. His visits were quite rare, too, as he lived at Toft Hill, the next village up the valley, and kids from one village almost never ventured into another alone, although the only person who ever tried to shoo Geordie out of Witton Park was bashed for his trouble. Geordie always stood near the Top House pub, scrutinising the plates of passing cars and making jottings in his thick, blue notebook.

Jack arrived back at the village long before the rest of us and smiled at Geordie.

"Now, kid!" he said.

"Hello," came the simple reply. Approaching Geordie was always a bit of a gamble, so Jack quickly flashed him a piece of paper upon which he had noted the number of the car that had passed us on the bridge.

"Betcha don't have this one Geordie!" he said. Eagerly Geordie perused the scrap of paper and said triumphantly,

"B'longs to Mr. Graeme, from West Auckland!" he beamed. Jack looked sidelong at him and said,

"Can't do, Geordie. I've just seen another fella driving it up the New Road."

Geordie was offended. "He musta nicked it then," he said, "'Cos it's not his!" and with that he stormed off toward Toft Hill.

Now this had a strange effect upon my brother, as he took the statement quite literally and decided that the vehicle had indeed been stolen, and today was a good day to turn gumshoe and do a bit of detective work. When we met up with him he told us the story of this man—the one on the bridge—and of how he had robbed Mr. Graeme of his car, and how he was now 'at large' in the village and perhaps (most exciting of all), there would be a reward for his capture. He was very convincing and we were intrigued by this mystery and, of course, eager to pitch in and clear it up.

The sun did not disappear at that time of year until after nine, so we had lots of time between tea and bed to do some sleuthing. Everyone was up for it. Jack was visibly irked at Roger, who appeared with a little note pad and the two-inch pencil that my dad used for writing out betting slips. He looked really professional and it annoyed Jack, most especially when Roger licked the pencil and wrote things.

"What you writing?"

"Things."

We had gathered in the lengthening shadows in front of the general store—Nobby Clarke, proprietor.

"We have to find out who this man is," said Jack. He began to pace back and forth, with his hands behind his back. He looked good.

"Obviously," he continued, "Obviously he's a criminal. Jus' got to look at him, right?" We agreed.

"Secondly," Jack paused, racking his brain to substantiate the accusation, "Er...we better have him followed!" Excellent! We all volunteered and were not to be put off by Jack's insistence that we would be spotted in such a large bunch, so, upon promising to keep quiet and maintain a low profile, we trooped along behind big brother in search of the pale blue Morris Oxford and its strange driver.

We started the search by doing a round of the public houses— they were always fertile hunting ground for men older than eighteen. It was almost opening time and many of the older fellows were already gathered outside of their favourite toping-posts. The old men were kind and laughed a good deal. They talked of hard times and ill fortune, which we did not understand, not having shared them. Nearly all of them sucked peppermints, again I knew not why. Indigestion, perhaps or to tone down the cheery beery bouquet of their breath before trotting home to the wife. Anyway, we all managed to cadge one from the old boys, and asked too if they had seen the car. The replies ranged from a simple 'no' to things as far fetched as '...oh, yes, I think I saw the Duke of Edinburgh drivin' it along the embankment jus' now.' Still, we took it all with a pinch of salt and moved on to the next place. The next place was pretty much like the last and it seemed that we would never find the man.

"Why don't we split up?" I said. I do not know why it took so long to think of it, but now that it came to be mentioned everyone thought it a good idea and we divided our talents into two groups. Nobody wanted to search alone so we had to have one pair and one group of three. It would have suited the others admirably to be in pairs and to leave me behind.

"Too noisy," they said.

"Laughs too much," they said. I suppose that they were right. I could not help it, though. To this day I laugh at the slightest little thing, more especially when it is least warranted. I did feel, however, that these small quirks were well under control, and were it not for my shoulders bobbing up and down like mad, one would never know that I was having a giggle attack. As usual I begged and crawled and ended up as one of the duo with Roger. Jack had done this deliberately as a retaliatory measure for Roger's scribblings that he felt had diminished his authority.

"What you writing?" I ask Rodge.

"Things," he says.

We set out in the direction of St. Chad's school and the others went to the opposite end of the village with the intention that we would meet up at Violet's fish and chip shop in the middle. Rodge and I stopped to inspect the contents of Mary Mac's sweetshop window. Mrs. MacDonald also sold home knit cardigans and baby clothes and, because the window faced south and caught the sun all day, it was protected by a green tinged plastic drape that was quite difficult to see through. We had to press our faces to the glass and blinker our eyes with cupped hands.

"What's your favourite?" said Roger.

"Coconut-ice," I replied without hesitation. "What's yours?"

"Sports mixture." These were hard gums in the shape of various pieces of sporting equipment.

"What colour?"

"Red, no, black." We were both drooling but did not possess a penny between us. As luck would have it, Mrs. Mac was a good friend of the family, and at that moment she called us in and gave us each a gobstopper. Mine was green to begin with, but went pink almost immediately. Preoccupied with these changes, and thanking our benefactor sincerely for her kindness, we did not notice the man who entered the shop until he spoke.

"Packet of cigarettes, please." It was *him*. Roger went white and I thought the gobstopper had lodged in his throat so I whammed him in the back. The ball shot from his mouth and bounced on the tiled floor. With two skips it cleared the doorway and took off down the front path. We ran after it, thankful for the excuse to leave. It came to rest at the edge of a flowerbed where we caught it up.

"We'd better get the others," said Rodge as he rolled the gobstopper around his mouth to remove the dirt that he subsequently spat onto the ground. "You stay here and I'll be right back!" He was gone before I had had time to think or even to ask what I was supposed to do if the man was to leave. True to form he did just that as soon as my brother turned the corner out of sight. He even said hello. Then he smiled and crossed the street to where the blue car was parked. As he reached for the handle he stopped and snapped his fingers as though he had forgotten something, then turned and retraced his steps back to the shop. I crept over to the car, determined that he should not leave.

Meanwhile, the rest of the gang was returning, and with them they were bringing an unwilling policeman, P.C. Pinkerton. They had almost convinced the bobby that something was amiss with this character, and he had reluctantly succumbed to their pleas and had "... accompanied to investigate." The man re-emerged and blankly stared at the posse before him.

"Hello," he said again. "Can I help you, officer?"

"Er, yes," began P.C. Pinkerton, somewhat embarrassed. "Er...would you mind telling me why you are driving Mr. Graeme's car, sir?"

"Well, yes," said the man with a smile. "He's my brother and I'm using the car while mine gets repaired." The entire throng went quiet and the policeman began to redden as he perused the driver's licence offered by the man. Either his embarrassment was increasing or, more likely, he was beginning to fume at having been stupid enough to believe my brother's tale.

"Thank you, sir. Sorry to bother you." he said.

"Not at all," came the pleasant reply. The policeman turned and cast a fierce glare at my brothers and I chose that moment to return from across the street. I announced with great pride into Jack's ear,

"He's going nowhere! I just let the air out of all four of his tyres."

The Conker King

It was a one of those natural events that arrives so suddenly it seemed magical. The late rains had filled the fruit in the orchards and apples were ready for picking. Nutty Wicker appeared at our back door one day asking if we'd like to buy a few pippins.

"Where are they from?" asked my dad. Nutty touched the side of his nose.

"Say nowt," he whispered. "A gift of Mother Nature." And he flashed that enormous smile that made other people smile with him. One of the things that endeared Nutty to the villagers was the way he was always in step with the seasons. In the spring, he waited for the first snowdrop to push through and defy the cold weather. Nothing was more important to him than how quickly new growth came; he timed everything by greenery and not by weather forecasts and calendars like other people. In summer, he was difficult to find as he spent a great deal of time wandering in the woods, along the river and up on the moors marking the position and progress of all the plants that he used to make a living. But Nutty really came into his own in the late summer and autumn when he gathered all his ingredients and turned them into jam, wine, soap, brooms, folk-medicines and pagan idols. When the wheat was harvested, Nutty made little corn dollies and tied them to bushes and trees all over the countryside and if you looked really carefully, you could find them nailed up around the village; in dark corners of hen houses, under the railway bridge, above the door of the pub and he always enraged Father McShame by pinning one to the parish notice board.

"He might get away with this with the Anglicans but I will not stand for it!" McShame told my dad. But it never stopped while I lived there.

"Listen," said my dad. "These apples aren't nicked are they? I mean I've had the priest around complaining about you again and I don't want to offend him." I sat quietly down on the upturned rain barrel and eavesdropped. I enjoyed conversations between my dad and Nutty. There was always something under the surface of them that I could not understand, but it was always amusing.

"George," said Nutty. "I don't steal things, you know that." My father raised an eyebrow.

"Maybe you and I have different views on what stealing is... I know you don't mind helping yourself to holly and mistletoe when the time's right." I looked back to Nutty as though I were watching a tennis match.

"I get my Yule greenery from the same trees every year. It wasn't me that built a wall around them and called it private land." He had a point there as the owner of the property—Zebedee Scott, the absentee landlord whose family had owned the failed local coalmine—fenced in the trees solely to keep us kids from scrumping his apples which I too felt was an injustice. Scrumping was our word for, well, stealing, but it's sort of traditional isn't it?

My dad wasn't convinced and refused to buy the apples.

"If it's because of the father you won't have to put up with it much longer," said Nutty. "He's been posted to the new town with the rest of the sheep." My dad's mouth fell open.

"Sorry if you didn't know George, a little bird told me. Anyway, I'll be off. See you later." And before he left he pointed to my chest and said, "What's that?" When I looked down he ran his finger up to my nose, tweaked it and we both laughed.

"Have a pippin," he said lifted the sneck on the back gate and disappeared through it.

It seemed that Father McShame had been given permission from the Bishop to move to Woodhouse Close with his parishioners and had done an about-face. Even as I made an awful noise eating the apple, he busied himself convincing his flock that things would be better in the Promised Land. Dad was wearing his worried look. I knew that his campaign to keep us in the village would be in big trouble if the priest left. What would a church family do without a leader? He pushed his hands deep into his trouser pockets and looked down at the ground. I decided to leave him to it.

"I'm off to get some conkers, Dad."

"Right," he said. "Just be careful and stay out of trouble."

I walked up the bank to the top of King Street and crossed Black Road. Outside the top shop I met up with Danny Bligh and Monty McBain. They already had a two dozen or more horse chestnuts and were busy poking holes through them with a knitting needle.

"Now, kid," said Danny. "We've got conkers! If you gimme a hand to get the string threaded I'll give you a couple." No need to ask twice. I put my brain to work immediately and suggested we put the conkers on the floor so we could really lean on the knitting needle and shove it through. The nut-brown chestnuts slithered through our fingers as we planted them in the grass. Danny leaned on the needle and it bent double with no effect at all on the conker.

"Pigging Nora," said Danny. "Your mother will go mad when she sees this needle." Monty McBain shrugged his shoulders and we straightened it out and tried again.

"Turn the conker over and see if it goes in any easier from the other side," I suggested. It did just that and we were in business. Danny pulled lots of string from the same paper bag the conkers were in and took a few minutes to bite it off at appropriate lengths. Then he knotted the ends and threaded a conker onto each string. This took a while as the ends of the string were very frayed and wouldn't go through the rough-edged holes without a good deal of swearing and threats. Danny had one eye closed and his tongue poked out of the right side of his mouth through the whole operation.

Once we each had strung conkers, we drew straws to see who played first. As Danny drew the short straw, he reversed the traditional rules and went first against me. I held out my conker and he took an enormous swipe at it, missing by at least a hand's width.

"Tipped it!" he said quickly. I dared not argue. He swung again, missed and caught me hard on the back of the hand. As I howled in pain, he said I'd moved on purpose and drew my hand into the ready position once again. A purple bruise was already glowing on my skin. This time Danny gritted his teeth and I was fearful he'd break a bone.

"Skinchies," I said, withdrawing the outstretched conker. "I'll just let out a bit more string." And I loosed another few coils so that the conker swung well away from my body and, more importantly, my hand. There was a mighty rush of wind as Danny thrashed his conker against mine, a loud crack and bits of horse chestnut flew everywhere. We had all closed our eyes for a second, but upon opening them I was delighted to see my conker still intact and Danny's string hanging limp in his hand.

"Right then," I said. "Mine's a one-er. Are you ready?" And I turned to Monty McBain who looked on in disbelief. He held out his conker and I gave it a really good whack but it didn't break. He smiled and looked at Danny. I held out my conker. Now, that conker was nearer to him than it was to me but he managed to hit me on exactly the same spot Danny had. They laughed like hyenas as I jumped around holding my hand to my mouth and eased a stifled cry through clenched teeth.

"Did you do that on purpose?" I demanded, but Monty McBain just shrugged his shoulders and held out his conker. I took a good, long wind up and swung. Crack! His conker exploded into a dozen fragments and I became the proud owner of a two-er. I couldn't help but smile and the pain from my growing bruise subsided just a little. Danny produced a second conker from the bag. He fixed me with a mean stare and held out the shiny brown target. Just as I swung he moved ever so slightly backwards and the conkers didn't connect.

"Ha! Missed!" he cried in delight.

"You moved!"

"Did not," he said matter-of-factly. "Hold it out." I duly obliged. The first swing entangled the strings and Danny cried 'slings' before I could claim 'no slings.' He swung again. This time there was a resounding crack and we examined our conkers. Neither seemed any worse for wear. He swung again and a tiny split appeared on his. The next swing missed and it was my turn.

"Skinchies," said Danny, and turning away he dipped into the bag and produced yet another conker.

"That's not the same one," I protested. "You can't switch in the middle of a match, Danny. It's not fair."

"Yes it is the same one," he said. "I was just wiping something off it." The new conker was at least twice the size of the one he'd first held out and I knew there wasn't much point in arguing. I took a swipe at it and again he moved it away.

"Danny..."

"Yes?" he said, planting his feet wide apart and glaring at me fiercely.

"Nothing."

I held out my conker and he swung. Double delight! He not only managed to miss my hand this time, but his new conker lay on the floor cleanly split in two. This time I held back the smile and just said, "Oh, bad luck."

"Give me another," he said to Monty McBain. After half-an-hour I had smashed all of Danny's conkers, all of Monty McBain's and even my own spares which Danny had commandeered. I was packing a twenty-seven-er. Danny stepped up to me when the last of his cache bit the dust and I half expected him to lay claim to my champion. Instead, he smiled and suggested we go scrumping.

"Right," I said, not wanting to annoy him. "Skeet's?"

"Of course."

A Scrumping We Will Go ...

There was only one apple tree in Witton Park that I could climb and it stood in the orchard at the back of Skeet's, the largest house in the village. During an affluent period—for most Witton Parkers that occurred on a Friday in May of 1868—the rich mine owners, doctors and Anglican clergy had moved into beautiful houses built of off-white brick along Main Street at the south-eastern edge of the village. Over the years, the Victorian mansions became covered in cool-green ivy and the red beech trees, planted when the houses were new, grew together to provide shady seclusion from the squalor of the rest of the village and an effective barrier between the rich and the poor.

Ironically, the only other landowners in the village were the tinkers who kept their ponies on a paddock that backed right up to the mansion gardens. It was fenced off, of course, by hedges of tall privet or in some cases thick, emerald box. We had found every accessible gap in this barrier over the years and getting into the property was easy. Danny Bligh dropped to his hands and knees and took a looksee into Skeet's orchard.

"The dog's out," he said, smiling. No one took Skeet's little dog seriously. It was a Pekinese and looked very much like an animated moustache. It couldn't bite very well but it was a yappy thing and was already making an awful commotion at the other side of the hedge.

"C'mere little dog," said Danny as he bent down to look through a hole in the hedge.

"It's called Chuckie-boots," said Monty McBain.

"Not by me it's not!" said Danny.

"Not by us it's not!" I added.

The curious dog came snuffling to Danny's fingers and he stroked it a few times before picking it up. He ran all the way along the paddock until he was at the last house. I made a telescope by curling my hand into a loose fist and peering through the tunnel it made. Danny seemed miles away but as I watched he carefully dropped the Pekinese over the fence into someone else's garden and hurried back.

"Solved that," he said, smiling. "Now, somebody has to go through the hedge first." We looked at Monty McBain and he knew what was required. Down he went and shuffled through the gap like a mole on the trail of a lobworm. I waited a few moments—in case he got caught—then I too went into the orchard. Danny came in last and without instruction we all began to pick up apples from the ground.

"These are pretty bruised," said Danny. "Get up the tree and get some good 'uns," he said.

"I went through the gap first," said Monty McBain. "So he should shinny up the tree." I couldn't argue so I grabbed onto the lowest branch and swung my legs upwards. Bits of silvery-grey bark showered down from the tree and I was forced to close my eyes until I was sitting on the branch and could rub them. I was also covered in green moss and shards of leaf, which in the minds of apple scrumpers and the people who manufacture soap powder is a good thing.

"The best ones are right at the top," called Danny. And that's where they'll have to stay, I thought. I climbed higher anyway and began to drop the grass-green apples to the boys below. The biggest of these hit a branch on the way down and burst at one side. Danny picked it up and bit into it.

"Don't throw them," he said. "Carry them down or they get bashed." Easy for him to say but I had no bag to put them in. I looked at my Fair Isle sleeveless pullover and wondered how much it would hold. Leaning back against the trunk I pulled the front of my sweater into the shape of a basket and placed apples in it with the other hand. It might well have held a couple of dozen, but there were only about fifteen within reach and as I wasn't prepared to take the risk of a sudden fall from grace, I decided fifteen was quite enough.

Even gathering those proved difficult. I had to inch my way along the branch for the first three and then up and to the left to get more. As I stepped onto the third branch, almost at the back of the tree from where I had begun, a twig pointing earthward stuck into the top of my head and caused immense pain. If I hadn't been afraid that Monty McBain and Danny would think me a cry-baby, I would have yelled blue murder.

By the time I had manoeuvred myself into a safe position to reach the last of my cache, I noticed it had gone very quiet below. The persistent babble that had been in the background since I started this climb had suddenly stopped and the silence was a louder warning of danger than any pre-arranged signal could have been. I cautiously peered over my shoulder and down to the foot of the tree. And, to use my mother's colourful expression, my heart leapt into my mouth. Far below I could see clearly a bird's eye view of the local bobby, P.C. Pinkerton.

Pinkerton was half stooped over, checking the long dry grass for signs of apple scrumpers, but my two comrades had obviously seen his approach and legged it without being caught. On the other hand, I was still in the tree. Thanks, lads. I kept as still as I could. If I didn't move he might never look up.

Pinkerton looked up. I almost died and was on the verge of coming clean when he looked away again. Somehow he hadn't seen me. I guessed that the sun overhead and the foliage had made me difficult to spot and I was thankful for it. By the rules of boyhood chivalry as they applied to Witton Park, this meant that I could lay claim to all the apples and was under no obligation to share them with my two absent accomplices. I was glad about that, although I fully intended to give them a share anyway, partly because it would make me look good in Danny's eyes and partly because I knew I'd never be able to eat them all myself.

As I was thinking about this, I noticed a really big apple out at the end of the branch below me and was making plans to gather it on the way down as soon as Pinkerton left. Even as I watched, a breeze came up out of nowhere and the apple began to sway. Back and forth, back and forth, until at last it separated from the leaves around it and fell to the ground right between P.C. Pinkerton's big flat feet.

"Right," he said calmly. "Come down from there. Right now."

There were two bobbies in Witton Park: Pinkerton and his jovial colleague P.C. Tubbs. If there had ever been a fitness requirement to get into the police, Tubby must have somehow avoided it. He was almost as wide as he was tall and whenever I heard 'The Laughing Policeman' on the radio programme Children's Choice, I always thought of him. He never arrested anyone and I heard many years later that he had been put behind a desk because someone noticed that he had not so much as written a parking ticket in all his years on the force. He once told me that he was going to walk up to the corner of Thompson Street and how he hoped no one was taking bets there... of course I ran ahead of him and told all the old codgers what he had said. They dispersed before he arrived.

Anyway, if you were going to get caught performing mischief, Tubby was the copper of preference. Just my luck to get Pinkerton, who had not—during my lifetime—ever cracked a smile.

"Thieving are you?" he said in a cold tone.

"No, sir," I said. "I was just gathering windfalls."

"Up the bloody tree?" Good point. He had me there. He stretched out a hand and pulled my jumper up and down. All the apples tumbled to the ground and I was reminded of a Movietone-News scene where the Nazi guard had caught a Polish kid smuggling carrots into a ghetto. Pinkerton then took hold of my ear, twisted it through 360 degrees and dragged me to Skeet's front door. He gave it the postman's knock. When it opened, a woman dressed all in black peered around it with a scared look on her face.

"Yes, officer?" she said in a small voice.

"Good day, missus," began the policeman. "I found this boy in your orchard stealing apples."

"What were you doing in my orchard?" she asked him. Both Pinkerton and I opened our eyes at the sharpness of her question. "I'm a police officer, madam..."

"You've got no right in my garden," she insisted, "Get away now or I'll have the law on you!"

"I am the law..." said Pinkerton.

"You're just a bobby," she countered. "The chief justice is a personal friend of mine! Now leave this boy alone!" And she grabbed me by the shoulder and hauled me into her hallway, slamming the door loudly. Through the frosted glass I could see the hazy outline of Pinkerton remove his helmet and scratch his head as he moved off. I was terrified. What on earth was a chief justice?

She took me into the living room and I was awestruck at all the nifty stuff it contained. It was just like a movie set: old fashioned furniture, candlesticks, stuffed animal heads protruding through the walls and in the corner a giant elephant's foot umbrella stand complete with ivory-handled parasols and huge black brollies.

"You can leave the back way once he's safely out of the picture," she said. "I'm Mrs. Skeet." She held out her hand and I hardly knew what to do. I took it and waggled it a few times.

"Goodness... that's no way to shake hands! Here..." and she grasped my hand tight. "You have to be firm. Be sincere. No one likes a wet handshake... it's like being handed a dead fish." I shook her hand vigorously and she approved. She sat in an overstuffed armchair and looked me up and down.

"You live in the village?" she asked.

"Yes," I said. "But we might be moving."

"Is that good or bad?"

"Dad says it's none too swift, but Mam is keen." I said. She laughed and I felt a bit more comfortable. She looked much younger when she laughed than she did when she frowned. You'd never believe she could see a bobby off.

"I hate it here," she said flatly. "I was brought here from Cambridge twenty years ago and abandoned. Do you know where Cambridge is, little boy?"

"No," I said. And I wasn't sure what abandoned meant either. I had this vague notion of little women and children climbing down her ringlets into tiny lifeboats.

"My husband's family owned the mines around here. And the iron works. Surely your father must have worked for him. Everyone did."

"My dad works for the railway," I said proudly. "We get free rides all over the place. Well, we only get one free ride to the seaside at Redcar each year because my dad works all the rest of the time."

"I thought the railway was closing down," she said. That was news to me and I think she saw it in my face. "Is Redcar nice?"

"Smashing," I said. "There's shrimps and tea on the beach and we get to sing songs on the train on the way home and my dad plays '*Isle of Capri*' on his harmonica."

"How nice."

"It is, except we always take tomato sandwiches and they get soggy before we can eat them." I felt I was doing really well and hoped she'd invite me to pick up all the apples I'd had to leave on the ground. She read my mind.

"You may take one of the apples with you. And please don't climb the trees. Fruit trees are very easily damaged you know."

"Sorry," I said.

"Don't say sorry unless you mean it," she wagged a finger in my face. "Men are always saying sorry. Why don't you just stop doing whatever it is you're sorry for?" I had no idea what she was talking about and began to worry that I might never get out of that house. Pinkerton was long gone and I suggested I move along too.

"I have to go home for my tea now," I said.

"Tell your father he's very lucky to have a choice," she said, brightening.

"I will," I said. As if! How could I explain why I'd been in Skeet's house in the first place... 'Hey, Dad, I was just pinchin' apples and weird Mrs. Skeet said to say hello...' I turned the handle on the front door and stepped outside. She was very nice, but I was glad to be free again. She closed the door without saying goodbye. Of course I took no notice of her telling me I could have one apple— it didn't seem right that she owned hundreds and was willing to let them rot before she's give them away. I stuffed my jumper with as many apples as I could carry. No point in letting them go to waste. I was wondering how I was going to slither under the fence without spilling my cargo and suddenly it occurred to me that I could walk out through the front gate. I had hoped that Danny Bligh and Monty

McBain would see me leave and I thought about inventing some fantastic story they could marvel at, but getting one over on P.C. Pinkerton was good enough for me. And it would no doubt impress the two of them. As I closed the gate behind me, I took one last look at the great house and felt just a bit sorry for Mrs. Skeet who wanted to leave and had to stay. Still, she had lots and lots of apples.

Bonfire Night

Guy Fawkes night. Ah, what magical vision leaps forth at the very mention! Gone now are the lax ways of the past that allowed anyone to purchase fireworks, child or madman, it mattered not to the vendors of such devices as squibs, jumping-jacks, or the ear-shattering tuppenny cannon. Come one, come all, celebrate the eleventh-hour unearthing of the treacherous gunpowder plot! Of course the political motivations of the traitors didn't enter into it. Kids never knew and kids never cared. There was only one question that concerned us: Johnny or Gardener?

John Street and Garden Street hosted the village's rival bonfires, and the reply to the 'one question' was usually tailored to match the allegiance of the asker, careful and correct assessment of whom could save one considerable strife. I learned this life-skill from my grandfather who diplomatically agreed with anyone who was looking for an argument; a ploy developed chiefly to avoid lengthy confrontation with irksome callers. It was for this very reason that he held both the presidency of the temperance league and the captaincy of the yard-of-ale team at the Welsh Harp pub.

It seemed everyone in the village was allied to either John Street or Garden Street; there were no neutrals and the rivalry resulted in two huge bonfires in respective derelict areas. Neither was significantly superior to the other, yet year after year both parties suffered the pilfering, destruction and sabotage of the other. One year, the Garden Street bonfire was lit in October by some night-skulking arsonist and had to be rebuilt from scratch. Fights broke out. Fences, gates and doors mysteriously disappeared only to re-emerge as kindling in the depths of the bonfires and all the while a seemingly constant movement of small boys, looking for all the world like leaf ants, portaged bits of wood to add to the already mountainous collections.

"Johnny or Gardener?"

I looked up from tying my bootlace and my eyes met with those of Spike Batty, local nasty.

"Erm..." I said, thinking. He grew immediately impatient and waved an ugly-looking stick in front of me. "Johnny," I decided. Fortunately I had guessed correctly and to my relief he lowered the weapon.

"Good lad!" he bellowed as he slapped me in the back hard enough to bring tears to my eyes. "Come with us." It sounded half friendly but with an undertone suggesting there really wasn't a choice. I followed Spike and his entourage of the Scott brothers, Wee Walter Dobson and Biffer McNeal down Black Road toward the John Street bonfire that occupied its traditional spot atop the Eureka playing field. A camp had been constructed close by and we entered it with caution. Care had to be taken so as to avoid treading on unspeakable things that had been strewn around to serve as booby traps in case of an enemy raid. A dead crow hung from a bush; a pit containing something wet and smelly was camouflaged by placing thin sticks across it with a layer of straw on top—a spectacle visible for miles. All were successfully traversed.

Spike instructed us to sit down. We squatted either on hunkers or the yellowing sods of turf that had been cut days before and transported to this den. Spike walked to and fro like a high-ranking officer issuing a military briefing.

"Now then. Our bomfire..." he always said 'bomfire' "...is nowhere near the size of the Gardener's. What are we going to do?" His eyebrows shot up into his hairline and he looked straight at me.

"Well...er..." I began.

"I'll tell you what we're going to do," he went on, "We'll raid theirs and nick some wood." My stomach flipped. Someone always got hurt in these raids and I had an awful dread that it would be me. Spike ranted on about the 'plan,' issuing orders and offering strategies with the air of a seasoned campaigner, and all the while I was racking my brain to come up with an excuse that would preclude me from the fracas. I thought about saying 'my tea will be ready,' but not even I could lean on such a frail cop-out. In a flash it came to me. Seeing that I would be unable to get out of it completely I said quietly and seriously:

"I'll be the lookout. We need sharp eyes and I'm the best there is."

"Good lad!" bellowed Spike, whamming me in the back again," He's the best there is!" The others agreed. Not only had I managed to get out of the raiding party but had ensured that I would be advantageously placed to leg it if things turned ugly. And the boys thought I was great for doing it. It's true: there's one born every minute. Sometimes a fellow just can't go wrong.

We passed Beaker's old house on the way down King Street. The signs of abandonment were already evident. Yellowing newspapers grew old in place of curtains. Mrs. Beaker had been funny about her curtains. Mam said she had laced them herself. I wondered about that; it was an expression my father used to threaten a fabulous violence, which, thankfully, never occurred.

"If I find out you've been playing near the quarry again, I'll lace your backside!" I had vague pictures in my head of Beaker's mother whacking perfectly good sheers until they had holes in them. How did she get them so neatly patterned?

The front door, like other front doors in the village, was an outward sign of the order within, and Beaker's mam buffed her doorknob with religious fervour. The knob had been swiped, and in the maroon panel of the lower door, the legend 'PC loves FR' had been deeply carved.

"Round the back," said Spike.

"Where we going?"

"In here. There mus' be something that'll burn."

"But it's Beaker's house," I said.

"So? They've gone, haven't they?" Spike's voice was scornful. "They shifted ages ago. They took everything they wanted. We'll have what's left."

Spike was looking at me again. I looked at the dark house, glad the shadows would conceal our movements, and curious beyond curious. Round the back we found a window had already been punched out. Inside, all the floorboards in the living room had been lifted and removed.

"I wonder why they took the floor with them," I said.

"They didn't," Spike said. "My dad and Punk Powler had it last week."

Spike's dad and Punk were inseparable villains. I suppose they were always together because they could only muster enough savvy between them to function as a single unit. Their collective I.Q. only just made three figures. Most of the time they were not in gaol was spent trying to get there. Rookie detectives from Durham Constabulary were assigned these two to practice on. Three weeks after they stole the floorboards they used them to build a pigeon cree, high upon a hill, nice and visible. Portering the planks proved a dilemma for Punk, who could not quite decide whether they were comfier above or below his huge beer belly. Consequently, he dropped his end often. Spike's dad barked one final instruction before the bobby stepped from the bushes and pinched them:

"Punk, you silly bugger. Form one straight line behind me, an' watch where you're lookin'."

The house had a hollow feel to it; sounds were at the same time echoed and dampened. We spoke in whispers and were mocked by ghostly mimics hidden in corners and behind doors. Spike was immune to the dread that crept up my neck.

"Get a look around. Anything what'll burn." Before long he'd found a cardboard box on the shelf of a clothes closet in an upstairs bedroom. He hauled it down and we gathered to inspect its contents.

"Whoopee!" he said.

"Don't you think they might be coming back for this stuff?" I asked.

"No." Spike's knowledge of the world beyond the village was nil. Beaker and his family were somewhere on the dark side of the moon. There was some women's clothing including, to our delight, an enormous bra that Spike tied around one of the Scott brothers. Under the clothes were some magazines from New Zealand and Australia: A New Life Down Under.

"These will burn nicely," Spike said. I looked at the pictures of flowers and strange birds, so colourful that they even brightened the dim house. There was a teddy bear that we thought must have belonged to Beaker.

"What a girl's blouse," said Spike. He threw the stuffed toy onto the floor, stood on its torso and pulled off the head. "Jus' as I thought. This'll burn nicely, too."

At the bottom of the box was a bundle of letters marked 'British Forces Posted Overseas.' They were addressed to Beryl Chadwick at an address in Escomb, a village two miles down the valley. I knew Beaker's mother was called Beryl, and they were signed by someone called 'ever-loving-Tommy,' which wasn't Mr. Beaker's name. I told Spike, who couldn't read, that they were bills from the coal merchant.

"Great," he said, "Coals burn even better than wood."

I started to think about Beaker and wondered what he was doing at that moment in his new house on the new estate in the new town. Only a year before, his dad bought them one of the first televisions in the village and I was invited to watch Children's Hour sometimes. Of course he was just trying to be my pal, and I just went along with it to see their telly. I just pretended to like him for a bit. Just to watch telly.

The last thing to emerge from the box was a framed photo of Beaker when he was about three. He was wearing a bow tie and was sitting in this wicker chair with a great flared back. He looked really pukey.

"What a prat," Spike announced. Then he dropped the picture back into the box with the teddy bear and the letters. "Let's vamoose."

"I need a wizz," announced the younger Scott. He piddled in a corner and we left the same way we came in.

We made our way down King Street and on until we were standing by the church on Albion Street. Then, by winding our way across the top of Low Thompson Street we came into full view of the Garden Street woodpile. Less than a week remained before the big night and the tall structure was almost complete. It had taken a month to reach this size and its guardians were not about to let a gang of Johnnies make off with any of its fuel. Two rough-looking boys stood sentry between us and the bonfire. One held a long and very thick stick that he occasionally whirled around so that it cut the air with a menacing swoosh. The other was preoccupied with keeping warm and jumped up and down on the spot while flogging his upper body with his arms.

The evening was bitterly cold and each breath hung silvery in the air long after expiration. Jack Frost pinched mercilessly at our toes and fingers and we tried to make the latter warm by gently blowing on them then sliding them under each armpit. Noses ran and eyes were full of water and all in all we were a pretty miserable bunch. I wanted merely to turn about and go home to something warm. I knew that on the back burner of the stove in my house a large kettle of thrice-cooked stew was at that very moment bubbling slowly and I could almost smell it; as I envisioned the gravy-smothered dumplings floating on top my stomach gurgled aloud.

Spike, unfortunately, was determined to see the episode to the conclusion he had planned. He wanted to rush at the bonfire, grab what we could and leg it. I had reservations to say the least. Such a brash plan might result in someone getting walloped with that big club (and that someone might be me).

"If," I began, looking around for uninvited eavesdroppers, "If we can do it on the Q.T. and slope off undetected, well then, we can come back another night and do it again." The gang's eyes widened in unison.

"Brilliant!" concluded Spike once again mistaking my cowardice for cunning. He peered cautiously around the corner and thought for a minute. Presently his face went blank and his lower jaw dropped open; we all recognized the signs of thinking as they applied to Spike. One could be forgiven if, judging by the painful expressions, one thought he had solved the mystery of life; but no—it was merely another (the twenty-third, I think) amendment to the plan. He turned to the Scott brothers and made them jump.

"You two! Sneak down the back of Low King Street and then up Garden Street and start chucking stones at them two buggers there. As soon as they start to chase you we'll be in like Flynn and whip the wood!" His face produced a broad grin at the end of the sentence and for once it seemed he had come up with a good plan. I took up my position as lookout at the corner of the street and the rest waited patiently at the gable end of Thompson Street.

The daylight was fast disappearing and as I stood in the shadows there came the sound of the lamplighter, his boots crunching the cinder pathway underfoot as he made his nightly round. He stopped below a lamp and raised his pole to the ringed lever that turned up the gas flame. The soft yellow light fell around me and the old man looked over.

"Get away home, lad! Skulking about like that in the dark!" I moved off into the darkness, but as soon as he turned his back I resumed my original stance. The Scott brothers had commenced their taunting and the response was immediate. The two larger boys ran after them at once and they turned tail and fled in terror towards the railway station and away from the bonfire. They played their part well; abuse poured from them incessantly as their little legs churned in a blur. Soon the sounds were so distant that they were barely audible and Spike gave the signal to move in.

Cautiously and stealthily they moved forward; their leader turning and giving silent hand signals that sent them scurrying in various directions. Quickly and quietly they began a methodical plundering of the hard-won woodpile—being careful to remove pieces only from the lower centre so as not to leave it obviously depleted. They piled the loot to one side then went in for more. I was of the opinion that what they already had was sufficient but, being unable to communicate via mental telepathy, had to stand there and watch in silence.

Right in the middle of these proceedings I suddenly got a strange feeling, as though something bad was about to happen. Premonition, I believe it's called. Anyway, I couldn't quite put my finger on it and vaguely envisaged the collapse of the bonfire. I was sharply awoken from this daydream by a startling cold voice.

"Johnny or Gardener?"

All the blood drained from my face and it turned ghostly white in a second. My heart jumped into my mouth and began to pound so loudly that I thought I was going to choke. I slowly turned around and my fears were confirmed. There behind me were at least a dozen boys from the Garden Street gang. For the moment they were unable to see Spike and company, and they stood before me awaiting a reply. I cursed my ill fortune as I pondered the circumstances. After having gone to all the trouble of making sure that if anyone got caught it wouldn't be me, here I was in the midst of the enemy camp. How could I get out of this? Run? No. They would get me later even if I managed to give them the slip. Fight? Certainly not. There was only one thing for it. I lied.

"Quick! There's a bunch of Johnnies nicking our wood!" This did the trick admirably. They stepped around the corner and saw that I spoke true.

"What are you doing here? Are you their look-out?" The biggest of them had correctly guessed my role in the raid. I almost broke down and came clean but, fortunately, I was unable to overcome the urge to lie even more.

"Certainly not! I've been standing here for half the night freezing to death keeping an eye on these rogues and you accuse me of being one of them!"

"Sorry, pal..."

"Never mind sorry. The only reason I didn't try to stop them is 'cos there's loads of 'em..." I had made my point and they were too preoccupied at running headlong into a confrontation with the Johnnies to notice me melt into the shadows. As the cries and yells and oaths filled the crisp night air I quickly walked up King Street to the safety of the back kitchen at number nineteen. Standing with my back to the securely closed door I relaxed and drew in a deep whiff of the stew and dumplings.

"Piece of cake," I said. "Now to think up something Spike will swallow."

Mr. Gaitskill's Gift

When my dad's garden had given its all in the way of cabbages, it was customary to send Ned and me up to see Mr. Gaitskill.

Mr. Gaitskill, so Jack told us, was over a hundred years old and had only one set of clothes. His eyes watered constantly and he was as deaf as a plumb-bob. And if that wasn't enough, he suffered from what our parents called 'Parkinson's' and what we called 'the colly-wobbles.' But he was a true villager and would never see others go short. Sort of *mi cabbage es su cabbage*.

"Mr. Gaitskill!" shouted Ned, and in so doing set me off giggling until I got an elbow in the ribs.

"Ayah..."

"Shush..." Mr. Gaitskill didn't hear. He was busy pulling pea-canes from the frozen ground and throwing them onto a pile of what looked to me to be pretty neat stuff... glass cloches, pot rhubarb forcer and other things I didn't know the name or function of either.

"Mr. Gaitskill!" The old man turned around and wiped his eyes in a hanky as big as a pillowcase. Then he blew his nose into it and checked it out.

"Pardon?"

"Dad wants to know can we have a cabbage for Sunday dinner?"

"The bus doesn't stop here on Sundays," he said. That was it for me, my shoulders began to shake and I turned away.

"No, Mr. Gaitskill," Ned went on. " A cabbage, a cabbage."

"A cabbage?"

"Yeah."

"You want a cabbage, son?"

"Yeah, please." Mr. Gaitskill took a thin silver penknife from his pocket and pulled out the most substantial blade. It was a wondrous knife—even had a blade for getting boy scouts out of horses' hooves. Ned joined me in impossible attempts to stifle laughter when the old man bent down. His body shook as uncontrollably as ours and it seemed like he'd never get the cabbage cut. In the end, in his frustration, he pulled the plant from the ground, root and all. That stopped the laughter. Normally the cut was slashed with a cross so that new leaves sprouted. They never formed a head, but Mr. Gaitskill's rabbits depended on them for winter greenery.

"Tell yer dad," he said, "that after next week he can help himself. They're putting me in an old folks bungalow on the new estate." Ned and I looked at his face. There was nothing funny in him now, and I was sorry I'd laughed.

"They're pullin' this lot down first," he continued. He whittled the soil-clogged stem from the cabbage and discarded the outer leaves. Then he went on, not particularly to us, it seemed, pausing between the sentences.

"My missus is buried up yonder. Forty-one years we were married. Y'know them trees along the Bishop Road? They're poplars. One for every lad killed in the war. The Big 'Un I mean. Me brother Tom, me brother Bert. Ron and Len, me cousins. Me mates. They're cuttin' those down too. Forty-one years. They don't have gardens. Just winder boxes."

Ned and I stared at the ground. An insomniac beetle, half frozen, moved slowly over the bare earth. Ned picked it up and buried it under a handful of humus in Mr. Gaitskill's compost heap.

"Might as well let it die now, lad," said the old man. "They'll mash that thing flat next week along with everything else." Then he motioned us to follow him to the end of the allotment where he began to shake with excitement as well.

"Look here," he called, clapping his hands. "It's a little tree I've been growing." In between the water butt and a patch given frivolously over to still-blooming crysanthemums was the smallest Christmas tree I'd ever seen.

"You're a good kid, aren't you?" he said to Ned.

"Yeah," yelled Ned.

"Well, if you promise me something, I'll let you have this tree. Jus' dig it up—get yer dad to help—and keep it in a pot. Then, promise me, you'll plant it back in the ground after they've pulled me house down and flattened it all out. Promise?"

"Promise," yelled Ned.

"Right, then. You're a good kid tell yer mother." And without another word, he went back into his house, cabbage and all. Ned and I looked at each other.

"I got a tree," he said, genuinely pleased. I was jealous. I didn't even get the cabbage.

"Hey, lads!" came Mr. Gaitskill's voice. "Do you think your mam could do with a nice cabbage?"

"Well, that's what we came for really," I said.

"Pardon?"

"THANKS, MR. GAITSKILL!"

Good Will Unto All

"Ready?" Jack held his hands out, forefingers pointing up, elbows jutting out, ready to conduct the quire.

Good King Wenslus last looked out, on the feast of Ste-e-e-ven,

Rodge, Ned and Tim stood behind me at Nutty Wicker's front door.

When a snowball hit him in the snout, deep n'crisp n'e-e-ven.

The black sky was splashed in stars and our piping voices knifed the cold December night.

Brightly shone his konk that night, tho' the frost was cru-u-u-el,
When ole Santa Claus came in sight, sliding on a sho-o-o-vel.

Jack wrapped rat-a-tat on the door:

Chrissmus is comin', the geese are gettin' fat,
Please put a penny in the ole man's hat.
If yer havven gorra penny, a ha'penny will do
If yer havven gorra ha'penny God bless you!

The door opened and a warm yellow light washed over us. Nutty stepped out and smiled.

"What rosy noses! I can fix that," and he produced from behind the door a tin tray with fruitcake and elderberry wine. The wine was in small jam jars and he tapped the side of his nose as he passed it out.

"Mum's the word, eh boys? Say nowt to yer mam." I lifted the jar to my lips with the others and felt the purple potion warming its way through my plumbing.

"Waes hael!" said Nutty. "Have a bit o' cake." The cake was cut in finger thick slabs and weighed about twice what it looked.

"I made this at Halloween, " said Nutty. "Elderberries, hazels, brambles, apples...rum! Good stuff, good stuff."

"Better than pennies," I said during a brief break in the biting-chewing-washing it down orgy.

"Would you like to get a warm by the fire, boys?" Four of us were in favour and made moves toward the welcoming glow, but the idea was vetoed by Jack who wanted to get in as many houses as possible before the parental curfew kicked in.

"Thanks for the cake, Mr. Wicker."

"You're welcome."

"Thanks for the wine."

"What wine?" Nutty's door shut with a soft thud and I could hear his fa-la-la-ing as we shambled through the moonlight back toward the village.

As we passed the lower end of Black Road, what was left of the houses on Park Terrace was silhouetted against the Milky Way like broken teeth. Smashed bricks and mortar lay in tortured mounds by the side of the road.

"Look," said Tim. "It's the 'Little Darlin'.'" We scurried over the debris to take a closer look at the bulldozer that stood on the ravaged rubble, silently sentinel. It reminded me of a spider hovering over a cocooned victim. Rodge twisted the end of his flashlight and pointed the beam up at the machine. Below the operator's cabin was the infamous painting that Mam had forbidden us to look at. We moved in close and joyously pored over it. It was a naked lady with an abundance of mammaric grace.

"Cor," said Ned. "Look at those!"

"Not many of them to the pound," agreed Rodge. I couldn't help feeling that we'd get caught, but neither could I tear my eyes from the picture. Above the femme fatale, in gold letters shadowed in silver, were the words 'Little Darlin.' It looked just like the side of an Allied bomber plane. In the daytime, the bulldozer snarled and chomped its way through the condemned homes: bright, dangerous yellow and blind in its destruction. But here in the silent night it seemed very different.

"It's not so big as I thought," said Jack. "Not as big as it sounds."

"Let's get in and have a look," said Rodge, and, leaving me on guard, the others clambered up over the caterpillar tread and disappeared into the cab. I amused myself by shining the torch under my chin and making ghoulish faces.

"Look at all the knobs," said Jack.

"Look at all the dials," said Tim. "What's that one for?"

"Erm...revs," said Jack.

"Oh. What's revs?"

"Revs, stupid, *revs*."

"Oh, yeah."

When the beast had been well and truly scrutinized, the boys climbed down and gathered around me, and we shared out all the Bakelite knobs they had been able to unscrew. The machine had two huge quart-halogen lamps with peaked lids, giving it the look of half-closed eyes. The radiator grid formed a downward grimace, and the overall impression was of ill temper and menace.

"It looks like a devil," said Rodge. Rodge had this uncanny knack of saying stuff that gave me the willies. I found out that it was he who told Beaker that the sighing in the poplars was the cries of dead soldiers calling for their mothers.

"It looks," he continued, "like it's got its arms up and is gonna smash..." Here he trailed off, and I looked first to the raised bucket, then, in unison with my brothers, I looked at Ned. His face was blank, almost, like he'd been suddenly burnt and was in that split second of disbelief that precedes the pain. I looked back to the bucket. Mr. Gaitskill's little fir tree stood precariously at its lip; the top was broken over and its white flesh shone in the torchlight. The workmen had wrapped toilet paper around and around its base, and an empty cigarette packet stood in place of a Christmas star.

"I forgot to dig it up," Ned whispered. He spent a moment in thought, then bent over to pick up a stone.

"Go on, kid," said Jack. "Chuck it!" Ned did just that. It hit the side window and left a mark like a bullet hole. And that seemed to be the signal to send the rest of us scurrying for stones, bricks, bits of pipe and anything to repay in kind the cruel yellow monster.

"Excuse me," said Rodge. "I believe this is my dance." He stepped deftly up to the bulldozer and smashed out the amber fog lamp, then he offered the pipe to Ned, who inflicted the same fate upon both of the headlights.

"Having fun?"

"Smashing!"

There was venom in the destruction. I gritted my teeth so hard that my jaw ached afterwards. It was over quickly, like war it had exhausted our energies in a single burst.

"I'm shagged out," said Jack. "Cor, look what we did!" There was glass everywhere. Shards sparkled all over the bulldozer and carpeted the ground. We'd swiped all the knobs, and a bird's-nest of wiring dangled from the steering column. But the damage was superficial. It was obvious that the machine would fire up ready and willing in the New Year.

"We'd better scarper," said Jack. And scarper we did.

Once the frenzied flight got us a safe distance from the scene of the crime we stopped and held our hands over our beating hearts. Then came the panic about getting found out.

"Dad's certain to see all the glass and he knows we were up this way," said Rodge. "He'll ask and somebody'll give it away." Then they all looked directly at me. I can't think why. I could hold out against the old man for minutes on end. It was my mother's scrutiny I could not withstand.

"Why will he see it?" I asked.

"Because we're all going to midnight mass," said Tim. "And we pass right by here."

"It's clouding over," I said. "Maybe it'll be too dark."

"What about the street lamp?"

"We could smash it."

"What about the one across the road?"

"We could smash it."

"We've smashed enough, I think. Let's blame somebody else." Tim had arrived at the obvious solution and we bandied names for scapegoat selection. We first mulled over blaming Danny Bligh, but there was a chance he would be at the service, and we couldn't risk that. Ned suggested saying that Mr. Gaitskill had leaned against it and shook all the glass out. But, of course, he didn't live there anymore. In the end we decided to go with my more believable story: Billy Beaker had ridden the bus eight miles from his new home so that he could go carol-singing in the old neighbourhood and had been given too much elderberry wine by Nutty Wicker then had smashed up the bulldozer because he was drunk so don't bother asking him about it 'cos he won't remember then he got frightened and ran away and caught the last bus and went eight miles home. Who could doubt that? The general consensus of 'crap' didn't rattle my faith in it one jot.

The three or so hours between our getting home and setting off for midnight mass lasted for more than a hundred years. My grandfather's grandmother clock (I couldn't figure that one out either) marked the passing of time with a rhythm too slow to sing to. Jingle Bells was a dead loss. Even my dad's wax seventy-eights of smoochie Ink Spots were too upbeat for that tortuous timepiece.

"That clock's driving me batty," said Ned.

"We could smash it," I offered, and was immediately aware of my brothers' glares.

"Father Christmas doesn't come to little boys who smash things," my dad said softly.

"We already told him about Santa," said Jack.

"Oh," said Dad, seeming sadder about that than I'd been. "Well, no more talk of breaking things. There's enough of that going on around here without adding to it. Besides, your great-grandfather gave your mother's father that grandmother clock." (See? Told you.)

Finally, the time came to wrap up for the walk to church. We donned our woolly togs and slid our hands into mitts that had once been socks. Mufflers were twined around our necks and Balaclava helmets were tugged painfully past ears. Jack nudged me.

"Tell him."

"In a bit," I replied. I was determined not to say a word until actually pressed to do so. Perhaps the glass had been cleaned up. Perhaps Dad wouldn't see it. Perhaps I'd dreamt it. "Can we go the long way to church?"

"No," said Mam. "We'll miss the carols. You like to sing, don't you?"

"Yeah."

And with that, although we none of us realized it, the family stepped outside to walk for the last time to the midnight service at St. Chad's church. There was a silence in the night deep enough to convince me I was deaf, but upon raising my face to the sky I became joyfully aware of snowflakes falling fat and thick from the heavens. Already snow lay inches deep on the ground. Deep enough to make snowballs. Deep enough to slide in. Deep enough to cover little bits of broken glass and paint. Ah, the miracle of Christmas!

Snow Play

Most people were thoroughly sick of Christmas by the time Boxing Day drew to a close. Grown-ups came out of the coma they had eaten themselves into and the tinsel and trappings were stuffed back into shoeboxes until next year. Even the novelty of new toys had worn off and the outdoors beckoned again. I had been delighted that the snow had finally come on Christmas Eve and I'd been out in it every day since. After a two-week hiatus when the sky was empty and blue, the snow came back with a vengeance in mid-January. One morning Rodge opened the front door and stood in a near trance at what was before him.

"Dad," he called, "I think there's something wrong here..." There was a mad rush as we pushed past Dad in the hallway to get in on the intrigue. A snowdrift had blown up against the front door so that only a hand's width was left between the lintel and the white screen. Tim was the first to figure it out.

"Yahoo! It's snowed again!" and without hesitation he dived headlong through the wall of snow. As it happened, the snow in the drift had been whipped up from the pavement in front of the house and he landed on the almost bare and iron-hard flagstones with a muffled thud. The snow was still falling in fat flakes the size of postage stamps. While dad helped Tim up I walked out into the street with my arms spread wide, face to the grey sky and my tongue out.

Not far beyond where my brother landed, the snow was deep and soft and wet, the perfect kind for making snowballs, snowmen and igloos, and naturally, for sledging. Not since the soapbox had come to such a sorry end had we been to the pit heap, but I knew we'd be going that day.

"I'll sandpaper the runners, shall I?" asked Dad. "I wouldn't mind a go myself..." But he was out of luck there. Mam appeared at the front door and looked at the swirling snow.

"Right, you lot," she said. "Off out and play. This'll give your dad and me time to get the house tidy and back to normal." Before we left she made us 'bundle up' and what looked like Scott's expedition to the South Pole set of trailing the sledge behind us.

"Be careful," called Dad, and when I looked back he shrugged his shoulders and waved bravely before closing the door.

As soon as we were out of sight of the house Jack sat on the sledge and the rest of us became a four-man dog team.

"Mush," he said. And mush we did. Straight down the middle of Black Road, past the Eureka playing field and along the New Road to the pit heap. We weren't the first there; Danny Bligh and Alan Jimson were already racing belly-flap down the hill and Spike Batty was growing increasingly impatient with the cardboard box he was using as a sledge.

"Let's have a go," he said as he took the reins from my hands. But Jack pushed him away.

"Shove off."

I asked Spike if his cardboard was working OK and he cast me a sullen glance. He decided to leave the hill and as he passed by he whispered so that Jack would not hear, "I'll fix you for this." And he was off before I could ask what on earth I'd done. I wasn't too worried as Spike always made threats but the protection my brothers gave me meant he had never carried them out. Still, he didn't seem happy.

"Never mind him," said Danny Bligh. "He's just jealous because they won't let him move to Aycliffe."

"Why not?" I asked.

"Cos his da is a jailbird," he went on. "I heard them talking about it at the Top Shop." By 'them' he meant the quidnuncs and gossips who gathered at the grocer's on Black Road to delight in the misfortune of others. The latest piggy-in-the-middle was Spike's mother who had been refused a house on the new estate at Woodhouse Close and the one at Newton Aycliffe because her husband had a criminal record and was what they considered a bad lot. And he was, there's no denying it, only now the whole family was paying for his crimes. Poor Spike was never to reach the Promised Land and I for one was happy that the justice system worked.

"So he'll never come to Newton Aycliffe, not ever?" I could hardly believe my luck. No more Mrs. Trout, no more P.C. Pinkerton and no more Spike Batty. Could it get any better?

"No he can't come," said Danny, and then he dropped his bombshell. "We're not going either." I stood slack-jawed and stupefied. My best friend was not moving to the same town as I was. Could it get any worse?

"What do you mean? I remember your dad was one of the first to say he was going."

"We're going somewhere else," said Danny with a broad smile. "Somewhere even better." He stopped there and I almost died of curiosity.

"Well?" I demanded. "Where are you going?"

"South Africa," he said.

"Where's that?"

"I have no idea. But there's lots of good jobs and it's sunny. And there's black people too." Danny told us his Uncle Brian had gone there years before and now he had found a great job for Danny's dad and a house with servants and a swimming pool. Of course, no one believed him but that didn't alter the fact that they were going. One of the things I had looked forward to most at Aycliffe was getting into new scrapes with Danny Bligh. What was I to do now? My brothers were OK but it seemed they were always trying to get rid of me lately. South Africa was too far to take a bus and chances were, according to Danny, they'd never come back. I had no concept of never but it didn't sound good. I just hoped it didn't mean I'd have to pal around with Billy Beaker.

"Well," I said. "Maybe I could come and see the swimming pool sometime."

"Course you can," said Danny. "You're me best mate." And we smiled and got back to the lighter business of snowplay.

Sledging was one of my favourite things in the world in the winter. After Jack had had his dozen or so goes 'to make sure everything was in working order,' we took turns to scoot down the hill on the sledge. There were two schools of sledging, those who went down sitting, and those who went on their stomachs, or 'belly-flap.' I belonged to the latter, and for some reason it was deemed to be a much more daredevil mode than sitting. I couldn't see why, as there was little control over the sledge when you sat like a lump—lying down allowed you to trail your feet over the back and guide it around obstacles like tree stumps, other sledges and Alan Jimson. Oh-oh...

Alan had come a cropper on his last flight and suddenly he loomed right in front of me as I hurtled through the snow at what seemed like the speed of light. There was neither time to avoid him nor warn him of my approach and just as he got to his feet I swiped them from under him and he went buns over breakfast back to the ground.

"Sorry," I said once I came to a halt. Alan was lying on his back with the wind knocked clean out of him. He stared at the sky and wore a bewildered expression. At that moment he had little idea of what just happened. I used the opportunity to move off quietly and dragged the sledge back to the top of the hill and handed it over to Rodge, whose turn it was next.

"Nice driving," he said with a smile. "We ought to get this fitted out with a horn so's people will know you're coming."

"I never did it on purpose," I said. But I had an idea that Alan Jimson would not believe that. I looked to where he still lay in the snow and decided I'd better give him a hand up.

"Gimme a croggie to where Alan is," I asked Rodge.

"OK," he said, and laid down on the sledge so I could get on his back. Now, this wasn't any of my doing, but as soon as I jumped onto Rodge the other kids took it as sign to join in.

"Pile on! Pile On!" someone shouted, and half a dozen sledgers abandoned their own vehicles to crush my brother and I on our way down the hill. The sledge—almost predictably—headed straight for Alan Jimson, and though I implored Rodge to do something about it, and quick, we ploughed into Alan a second time and down he went again. This time he had the added misfortune to have several wet boys tumble on top of him, one of whom (me) ended up face to face with him at snow level.

"I knew it," he said. "I knew it would be you!" And he struggled to his feet and stood over me. For a moment I worried that he might do something nasty like tread on my head, but in the end he just shrugged in disbelief and went to retrieve his sledge. When he hauled it back to the hilltop, he wound his scarf close around his neck and tucked the ends down the front of his pants. He came over to me and I backed off just a little.

"Here, you can have it," he said. "We're leaving tomorrow. We're going to Australia. There's no snow there so I don't need the sledge." And he smiled as he handed over the steering rope. Then he held out his hand and we each of us shook it, just like grown-ups. As Alan Jimson turned away and slithered down the hillside, I crushed a handful of snow into a snowball and winged it after him. It hit him on the back of the head and almost all of it went down his shirt collar. He stopped for a moment and turned to look directly at me. Then he smiled and wagged a finger.

"You're a jinx, Philip," he said. "But from now on, you're somebody else's jinx." And he walked off without looking back.

Over the following hour, in dribs and drabs, all the other kids left the hillside, including my brothers, until I was the last left. As the sun went down and the hilltop was quickly shrouded in a black wrap, I sat alone on my new sledge and looked at the street lamps twinkling in the distant village. Danny was going to South Africa, Alan to Australia, Jennifer Mountjoy to Canada. It seemed so grand to be going to such far away places and I envied them a bit. But I didn't really want to go with them. Why couldn't everyone go to the same place? That seemed to me to be by far the best solution. But nobody asked me. If they had, I think I would have said, "let's just stay here." I straddled the sledge and, just to show I was as adventurous as any of those departing for distant parts of the Commonwealth, I zoomed down the hill one last time sitting bolt upright. The thrill of the ride through the pitch black drew my breath away and I discovered that I actually liked it.

As I walked home, my fear of moving ebbed and I began to look forward to Newton Aycliffe and all the adventures it would bring. I had hardly had time to get used to this new feeling of being the swashbuckling type when Spike Batty stepped out of the night and I just about turned inside out.

"Ha!" was all he said as he blocked my path by holding out his arms and opening his legs wide. He was grinning and it was all he could do not to laugh in his delight at having caught me alone. I couldn't check the colour of his nose because it was too dark, but I suspect it must have been blue because he had been waiting for me there since he left the hill hours earlier. Normally, I would have panicked, but things were changing. Instead of making a run for it, I surprised Spike—and myself—by smiling back at him.

"Here you go, Spike," I said, holding out the rope from Alan Jimson's sledge. "It's yours."

Pancake Day

When Shrove Tuesday dawned a watery light filtered through our bedroom window and we woke up with bright moods in anticipation of fun. Pancake day was always good for a laugh, especially as it preceded Ash Wednesday and that annual religious downer, Lent. Breakfast was to be boiled eggs and soldiers. My mother sawed off the heel of a farmhouse loaf and gave the knife to me.

"When you've cut that into slices you can take up some crusts to Kit Carson," she said. "Wait about and he'll give you an egg for your breakfast." We already had eggs, laid by Ned's chicken and her sisters in our very own chicken coop, but there was something almost magical about an egg from Kit Carson. I gathered the crusts from the previous day and put them in a brown paper bag. Bread was bought daily and went stale overnight so anything that wasn't eaten the day it was bought (which wasn't usually much) went in the bag.

Kit lived in a stone house opposite the place where Park Terrace had stood. The ground there was covered in a brave new growth of grass, fireweed and the ever-present dandelions. After the demolition crew left there had been little to pick over and the only sign that there had been human habitation at all was where the dirt had been compacted into a road. Kit had taken advantage of the situation by moving his chicken coop to the far end of the lot which was a good deal nearer than it had been on his allotment.

I placed the bag of crusts on his wall and called out.

"Some crusts for your hens, Mr. Carson!" Then I stood back and waited. It always took about five minutes to get a response from Kit, who had grown old and moved more slowly with each month that passed. When I had first been sent to deliver crusts I had thought he wasn't home as it took so long for him to put in an appearance. I had gone home again only for my mother to send me back to learn the virtue of patience.

"Good things come to he who waits," she said. And she was right of course. Just that I had to wait for what to a little kid was half a lifetime. When Kit finally did come out of his house he never opened the tall wooden gate to his backyard, nor said a word. A gnarled brown hand would slowly show over the top of the wall and take the bag away. Then it would reappear with an egg—brown like the hand—place it on the wall, and sink back in slow motion. In fact, I never knew what Kit looked like until someone pointed him out in the street months after I delivered the first crusts.

I took the egg, yelled my thanks and ran home. Maybe I imagined it, but I always fancied the egg was warm and laid in those five waiting minutes. It was placed in the pan by itself to boil, and very soon I was dipping toasted soldiers into it with delight.

"Well, today is the day for eggs!" my mother said. "There are pancakes to make and some for the race." Every Shrove Tuesday there was the bizarre ritual of racing from the post office to the front of the picture house while flipping a pancake in a frying pan. Only women were allowed to compete and the winner got a prize from the vicar and the title of 'Pancake Queen' for the year. Nutty Wicker entered every year dressed in drag and gave everyone a laugh. In years past lots of men had donned dresses and painted their faces to take part in the fun, but this year most of those who joined in had moved away and only Nutty was game.

"Shall you have a go this year, Mam?" I asked.

"Not this year," she said. "We've got company coming."

"Who's that then?" I asked.

"Mrs. Teesdale... she's the lady who interviews folks to see if they are good enough for Newton Aycliffe. She's on the town council. I'm hoping she can convince your dad that it's better than here. I hope he behaves... oh, and Aunty May and Miss McShame's coming too." Miss McShame was the priest's sister, no doubt there to influence Mrs. Teesdale's decision. Dad was still holding out on the move to Aycliffe. I had resigned myself to leaving the village by that time, although it had not really struck home. I had already told most of my friends that we'd be moving. I knew from experience that once my mother made up her mind it was impossible to shift her. All we were really waiting on was the official backing of Dad.

"Maybe the women'd like to join in the pancake race," I suggested. Sometimes my mother liked to wait to the last minute before she'd announce her intentions on things. I suspect my dad was waiting for her to change her mind about moving to the new town but she had seemed unshakable since Beaker told her about the factory with the big pay packets.

"I shouldn't think so," she said. "Aunty May weighs over fifteen stone and Miss McShame is almost blind." Oh well, I knew at least there would be a feast prepared. Aunty May only visited every few years and Miss McShame was the priest's sister down from Scotland to see her brother. For some reason the priest often brought people to see my mother. I think it had something to do with us being a large family and the fact that we were made to go to church lots.

"Now, off you go and watch them get ready for the race while I get on with things." I left the house and ran to the bottom of Low King Street where my brothers were gathered to cheer on the contestants. No grown-ups had arrived, but it was early and the women were doubtless still making the pancakes and the men were in the Welsh Harp drinking pints of Dutch courage.

"Guess what?" I said, and before they had a chance to reply I told them about the company.

"Great," said Jack, "That means there'll be stuff left over that we can have!" Mam always went overboard and made the sandwiches with fillings reserved for guests: salmon, special cheese and honey-flavoured ham. We usually got plain bread and butter or sometimes the treat of fish paste. Why she insisted on cutting the crusts off the guests' sandwiches I cannot say—they were my favourite part. Still, it meant there's be all the more for the exchange with Kit Carson the next day.

"Is Mam going in the race this year?" asked Tim.

"She sez no," I said, and they looked a little downcast.

"There's hardly anyone at all in it this time," said Jack. "It used to be great before everyone started moving away." He kicked a stone that skipped across the road and hit the kerb at the far side with a loud crack. "Do you remember when Dad dressed up and tripped over the dress he had on?" We laughed.

"And what about that time Beaker's mother was mad?" asked Ned. Beaker's mother had never entered the pancake race but that had not surprised anyone. Beaker's dad had once—and only once—turned up to race in the guise of a woman but she had taken him by the ear and marched him back home before they were under starter's orders. Nobody saw him for a week and the inevitable rumour that she had killed him did the circuit of gossips. But eventually we saw him creeping home from work one night and I remember I was glad he was still alive.

"Yeah," said Rodge. "It's not half as good." But just as the words left his lips the sound of tinkling bells made us all turn around. Coming down the street was the tallest woman I'd ever seen. She had a large hat covered in fruit: bananas, grapes, crab apples and all sorts of leafy things to make it look like a basket, and all around the rim hung tiny golden bells. She wore a bright red skirt which shimmered in the sunlight and was quite the most dazzling piece of clothing I had ever clapped eyes on. Her blouse was white and tied at the bottom so you could see her belly, which was—hairy! It was Nutty Wicker dressed as filmstar Carmen Miranda. Then we noticed the army boots and my brothers and I howled with laughter.

"Hello sailor," said Nutty, trailing a peacock feather across my face. "How about a little kiss?" He looked as though he had used an entire lipstick to redden his mouth and his eyes were shadowed in a bright pale blue colour that turned out to be snooker chalk.

"How do I look? Ready for the race?"

"It's not for another half-hour," laughed Jack.

"Well, then," said Nutty, sliding in small steps over the road. "I shall have to see if I can find any nice boys in the pub." And off he went to the Welsh Harp. We followed close behind and of course had to stop at the door, from where we heard a great whoop and lots of whistles from inside. I couldn't wait to be old enough to go to the pub, it always seemed such an interesting place.

People had begun to gather outside the post office by that time, although most of them, like us, were observers rather than participants. Early entrants included Annie Wilton, a perennial contestant who had won the contest more times than anyone else, Mrs. Beeton (no relation to the cookery writer), Miss Rowan, aging spinster of the parish and her sister, The Other Miss Rowan. Lots of small children were there too. Giggling, pushing and shoving in excited anticipation of the endangered village event.

I wondered if they had similar races at Aycliffe. I knew it was in England so surely they had Shove Tuesday, and what was the point in having it if there were no pancake races? When I voiced my concern Rodge said, "Hmm, maybe they just eat the pancakes..." Well, at least that made sense even if it was dull. Mentioning eating made me think of the pancakes we'd be getting from Mam after the race was over. I liked mine with syrup, or jam. Dad always had his with lemon, which I thought was very strange indeed. He could eat at least a dozen though, so he must have been keen.

Two girls in pinafores chalked a hopscotch pattern on the road and numbered the squares appropriately. We called hopscotch 'itchy-dabbers' and traditionally an empty shoe polish tin was filled with dirt or tiny pebbles and pitched onto the squares in ascending numerical order. As the first girl hopped from one square to the next the two of them sang back and forth:

"Pancake Tuesday is a holiday,
If we don't get a holiday
We'll all run away!"

"Where will you run to?"

"We'll run down the lane."

"I'll tell the teacher
And you'll get the cane!"

I wanted to join in but I knew my brothers would razz me. Mrs. Quadrini came out of the Italian ice-cream parlour and looked on the proceedings with a smile. Her husband was loading up their ice-cream cart with his wares and I went across to stroke Dolly, the horse. Dolly was trimmed up in festive ribbons and her brasses had been shined for the occasion. Sometimes, Mr. Quadrini tied a plume of red feathers to the top of her head, but on this day they were missing. Still, the horse looked very splendid and stepped forward onto my foot to show she too was in a merry mood.

"Ayah!" I barked, inadvertently joining the hopscotch after all. Horses weigh a lot and I thought for sure the skin had been scraped clean off my ankle. Mr. Quadrini gave me an ice cream cone in compensation for my injuries and I said thanks and went over to eat it in front of my brothers.

The men were coming from the pub with Nutty hoisted on their shoulders. They were singing the 'Parlez-vous' song—humming the rude bits—and laughing a great deal. Nutty carried a pint of ale aloft and sang at double volume. The vicar suddenly remembered something he'd forgotten to do and shuffled off to attend to it.

The crowd in front of the post office was by then worthy of the name, although it was nowhere near the size it used to be in years past. There was no need to jostle to get a good viewing position, and I for one was glad about that. Being the shortest person in a crowd usually meant I had to squat down and crawl between legs to get a decent shufti.

The contestants lined up, elbow out and frying pans to the fore.

"Good day, everyone," the vicar said, having considered it safe to return.

"Drop the flag!" came a voice form the safety of the crowd.

"It's nice to see such a good turn-out considering the circumstances..." continued the vicar.

"Drop the bloody flag!"

"Ahem... right then... without further ado, er..." the vicar pulled out a spotted blue hanky and waved it around. Off they went, amid squeals and cheers from the crowd.

"I say," said the vicar. " I didn't say go..." No one cared. It was brief and Annie Wilton crossed the finish line a clear winner. Nutty swanned his way along the course, brushing the feather boa in faces as he went. Half way down the course he flipped his pancake really high and a gust of wind blew it onto a rooftop. We loved that.

When the last contestant crossed the line (guess who) and the prizes had been handed out, the crowd dispersed and Nutty came over to us with a great grin on his face.

"I can't believe I didn't win anything," he said. "I must have been the best dressed!" He rummaged around in the black leather handbag he carried and produced a crumpled brown-paper package tied around with white string. "Give this to yer mother, Philip. It's po-po-ree."

"What's that when it's at home?" I asked.

"Well, it's just bits of dried flowers and stuff that smells nice."

"But what's it for?"

"It's posh. It's to impress people." Then I realized it should probably be in the parlour with Mrs. Teesdale so we'd get a good house in the new town.

"I'll take it home right now." I said.

"We'll come with you," said Jack, keen to get a look at what was going on in our house. We said hurried good-byes and ran off in a posse up the street.

The company had gathered in the parlour, our brightly lit front room that faced King Street. All children were banned from entering the parlour, which accounts for why it was the only room in the house that was always clean and tidy. The heirloom lace tablecloth was spread with several plates of sandwiches from which I could hardly tear my gaze. A bowl of black grapes, a tall pitcher of water and, of course, a large pot of tea snuggled in a bright woollen cosy. Toward the middle of the table, a three-tiered cake stand tortured us, bedecked as it was with Madeleine's, Eccles cakes and slabs of patchwork Battenburg.

We had been briefed before we entered: best behaviour, speak up; Ps and Qs and all that stuff. Mam was always afraid that we'd embarrass her, but especially so because of the calibre of the company that day.

"Good afternoon, John," said Miss McShame as she stepped forward to greet us.

"Good afternoon, Miss McShame," replied Jack politely. Mother smiled but it proved to be premature.

"Good afternoon, Roger."

"Mam says we can have anything you don't eat," said Rodge blankly. Mother let out an audible groan and shooed the rest of us out without a greeting back to the kitchen. She leaned forward and said in a harsh whisper, "I'll kill you." Then she went back into the parlour and shut the door. We exchanged shrugs and my brothers went back outside to play. I stayed on the off chance I could get in on the edible goodies.

It wasn't long before the door opened again and my mother came out to refill the teapot with boiling water and fresh leaves.

"Are the others out?" she asked, and when I told her yes, she let me go into the room with the guests 'so long as you don't come out with anything silly.' Well, not likely, right? I parked myself on a sit-up-and-beg chair between the fireplace and the couch where the women were. They asked me questions about school and church and I supplied the standard answers. Mam came back with the replenished teapot and put it on the table.

"Please help yourselves to sandwiches," she implored, but of course the ladies were not about to deplete the sandwich supply after my brother's comments. I could see my mother's eyebrows knit. She put Nutty's pot-pouri into a cut-glass finger bowl and placed it at the centre of the table.

"Please... perhaps a cake or biscuit..." She held out the plate so they could refuse no longer and each took a cucumber sandwich and an arrowroot biscuit. I wasn't offered anything, but if I had have been I would have gone for the ham and cheese, no contest. Everyone settled in and my mother poured more tea.

"I understand George has been offered the stationmaster's job at the railway," said Mrs. Teesdale. "That's a very responsible position."

"Yes," said Mam. "He's a very responsible type."

"Very responsible," added Miss McShame.

"It's just the kind of thing we look for in selecting tenants for Newton Aycliffe, but it's also a very good job... perhaps you have changed your minds about coming?" As Mrs. Teesdale took a sip of tea and my mother paused to consider the dilemma, the door opened and my dad walked in with the parish priest. A lot of handshaking went on, the men were given teas and stood in front of the fireplace to drink it. Dad took up the conversation.

"Yes, it's a great honour to be offered the job of station master," he said, bringing himself to his full height. "I've been with the railway since the end of the war, you know."

"End of the war," said Miss McShame.

"There's lots of variety. I get around quite a bit. All the signal boxes—Wear Valley Junction, Harperley, Simpasture Gate..."

"That one's near Newton Aycliffe isn't it?" said Father McShame.

"Yes," said Dad. "Right across from the plastics factory."

"I can make sure you get a job in the plastics factory," said Mrs. Teesdale. Dad looked lost for words. Mam looked elated. I looked at the sandwiches and wondered if the priest was going to eat the ham and cheese ones.

"Well, I'd be getting a pay rise at the railway," Dad said.

"The pay starts at twenty-five pounds a week plus bonus and lots of overtime at the plastics factory," Mrs. Teesdale countered. Twenty-five pounds was ten more than Dad got working for the railway and suddenly it was all over.

"Oh my!" chimed my mother. "We'll have a new washing machine in no time!"

"Washing machine," said Miss McShame.

"Gosh," said Father McShame. "That's more than I get on the collection plate in a month..."

I never understood Mam's obsession with washing clothes anyway. We just got them dirty again almost immediately. I could see how she'd have fun with a proper washer though. Just like the women on our recently-acquired TV whose lives were enriched by twin tubs and powder that got things whiter than white. And there it was written on her face. I saw it, and my dad saw it too—his face flashed three different signals one after the other: I could see him briefly search inside for something to say that would defend his position; then he looked at Mam and I saw the painful look of defeat; finally, his expression changed to resignation and he smiled as he embraced the inevitable. It was over all right, we were going to Newton Aycliffe.

"As much as that?" he feigned. "We could really start a new life with those wages, right Patsy?" And there it was: the official blessing. Before the last words were out of his mouth Mam had flung her arms around him and everybody was smiling. It looked like the last scene from a situation comedy, especially as Miss McShame was helping herself to a portion of pot-pouri in the mistaken belief that it was something to eat. Everyone was too polite to tell her, except me, but she seemed to be enjoying it so I heeded the 'don't-you-dare' signal in Mam's eyes and let it slide. The rose hips seemed particularly chewy. More tea was poured and plans were set in motion.

Dad was fairly quiet, preferring to discuss the job offer rather than compare the village to the town as Mam was doing with Mrs. Teesdale. Inevitably, the priest took the last ham and cheese sandwich and I laid a mild curse on him. Nutty taught me it—saying it only worked on priests and that it would make them think of something funny during a sermon. I never did find out if it worked, but sometimes when I thought about it, it made me laugh, so there must have been something to it.

In the end, the adult conversation became boring and I trundled outside at Mam's bidding to round up the gang. When I told them about the imminent move they split two and two, Jack and Tim embracing it and Ned and Rodge looking silently down the street as if they believed it would disappear any second.

"When will we leave?" asked Rodge.

"Dunno," I said. I had not much concept of time, except that I knew nothing seemed to happen fast enough unless it involved something I'd rather didn't happen. "Mam says we'll be there before the end of school term." None of us knew it, but that was just three weeks away.

"Did they eat all the grub?" asked Jack.

"All the ham and cheese is done for," I said. "But there's other stuff. And pancakes!" That's all it required. Thoughts of leaving dissolved, at least for a time, and we took off home to assist the company with all those beautiful little sandwiches and cakes.

The End

"What a sodding day to pick," said the driver to my dad.

"Well, it's now or never," he replied. "Anyway, a bit of drizzle never hurt anyone."

My mother insisted that the removal van arrive before the street was filled with neighbours. Recent experience during the exodus had taught her that a number of those who looked on had developed an uncanny eye for noticing the slightest imperfections in the furniture. Ours was old but carried none of the marks I'd seen on others. Danny Bligh had scratched his name on his mother's sideboard, to her surprise. Even Beaker had stuck wads of gum along the skirting of their best table. Of course, none of these shameful acts was discovered until the van men hauled them past the scrutiny of the neighbours.

That's the cupboard that used to be at the back of the church. I wondered where it went...look at the state of that table. Never had a cloth across it in years...those chairs are covered in cat hairs. The people who made the comments did so behind their hands and under their breath. I noticed that they were almost always women who took delight in knowing everyone else was as poorly off as themselves.

We had been woken up really early that day. Jack was charged with making sure I washed and dressed properly as Mam was too busy to supervise the usual routine. He handed this job off to Rodge along with a threat that in turn was passed on to me:

"Get washed and dressed proper or I'll thump yer lug."

"I always do it properly," I lied. This day was no different and I gave myself a lick and a promise and hurried to the breakfast table. Mother was too busy for this, too, and Ned was slopping milk all over the cornflakes at the kitchen counter.

"Where's the table?" I asked.

"In the van. So's all the chairs. We have to eat standing up." Ned had the only spoon and the rest of us were obliged to wait until he'd finished before we got to eat. I ate last. Dad and the van driver shooed us out of their way as they hurried back and forth with bits and pieces. Mother followed close behind and complained each time they banged a wall or scuffed a doorway.

"My mother gave us that. Please be more careful. George!"

"Yes, dear."

"Watch the staircase."

"Yes, dear."

"And hurry up."

I ate most of my cornflakes from the bowl like a dog, and after getting the last few with the spoon, I went to the front door to watch the loading of the van. A very large drop of rainwater fell in my eye when I looked up at the lead sky. Everything was subject to my mother's adjustments until the driver whispered something in Dad's ear. She was told then to take one of the boys and go on ahead via the bus to the new house. Tim was the one who went.

It was a strange departure, I thought. She was almost keen to get out of there. It took her no more than a minute to wrap up, grab her handbag and Tim, and step through the door.

"Before you leave," she instructed, "Check that both doors are locked, the water's turned off, the electric's off, the gas is off, the windows are shut and both doors are locked. Do you hear me? George?"

"Yes, dear."

"I'll get a fire in at the new house and I'll expect you between ten and noon. Right?"

And, not waiting for an answer, she set off toward the bus stop without a backward glance. She had been born in King Street during the depression, though the depression had been a permanent feature of village life. Now she stepped almost callously away from the home she had set up when she was newly wed. It gave me confidence that what was ahead must be something wonderful. I had heard our new house had a biffy upstairs and another down. I had heard that there was hot water all the time. I had even heard that I was to share a bedroom with only one brother, but I'd believe that when it happened.

Just before the time Mam left, and the van was almost half-full, kids from school began to filter past the house. They all stopped for a looksee and I proudly announced to each that we were moving to Newton Aycliffe.

"Where's that?" asked Margret Molloy.

"I don't know," I replied confidently. "But it's a long, long way from here."

"You'll be late for school."

"I'm not going to school."

"But it's gym today. They're picking sides for the footy team."

Of course! It was time to put on boots and play soccer—I couldn't possibly move today.

"Rodge," I said. "Today's the day they pick the footy team. Can we go tomorrow?" He put down the pile of shoeboxes and looked at me. He opened his mouth but nothing came out. Then he picked up the boxes again and looked for a home for them.

"Don't be stupid," said Jack, clagging my ear. "We're not going to St. Chad's anymore. We're finished. You'll be going to a new school." *You'll be going to a new school...* no one had told me that. New kids. New teachers. Well, I thought, I hope I get a better teacher than Mrs. Trout. Surely I would get a better teacher than Mrs. Trout?

"Are you coming?" asked Margret.

"No."

"I'm tellin' on you." She turned away and grabbed her little sister's hand and pulled it smartly. Half way up the hill from the house, she turned back and yelled through the veil of rain.

"Goodbye, Philip."

I was around the back of the house checking on the things Mam had mentioned when I heard, over the pitter-pat of rain, Foss Stanley's golden tones belting out the chorus of the latest hit – *I can't stop loving you...* far better than anything I'd heard from him before...*I made up my mind, to live in memory, of that lonesome time...* A minor miracle occurred on the verge of my departure. I had to investigate. Cautiously, I slipped the latch on Foss's back gate that was directly across the back alley from our own. By this time the alley had a small river running down its middle, making the place look like a poor man's Venice. A very poor man.

"Hello, Mr. Stanley."

"Is that Philip? Fill up me pint an' I'll sup it!" Gales of laughter. Same joke he always told. Foss always smelled of beer and he could belch loud enough to be heard three streets away. That, and the fact that he was always good for a sixpence if you met him on his way home from the Rose and Crown, made him a favourite with the kids. He saw the puzzlement in my face and smiled.

"Canny music, hey kid? Come an' look at the future." He ruffled my hair that fell forward over my eyes so that I looked like a rat peering through a storm drain.

"Gordon Bennett! You're awfully wet. Is it raining?" Foss took out a flattened five-pack of Strand cigarettes and lit one with a spill from a copper box on the hearth. The coal fire was lusciously warm, and I inched toward it as he waved an arm over what looked like a coffin on legs. Before he could say a word, he was thrown into a fit of coughing that made his eyes bulge and his whole body retch.

Hoar-r-r-k. Phtoo! He spat a lump of phlegm onto the coals where it sizzled and squealed.

"Ah, better out than in," he said as a matter of course. "Dust, kid, dust." Foss had been twenty years down the coalmines and the dust, a stoop, and permanent mascara were the most obvious signs of his affiliation. He waved again at the huge piece of furniture.

"Know what this is?"

"A box for sawing ladies in half?"

"High fidelity! All the way from Leeds. Made in the Yoo-nited States of America. How about that?"

"What is it?"

"It's a gramophone! There, look," he lifted a lid and I looked down onto the turntable. "You put the records here—up to six if you want—put this arm on top of 'em, turn this knob to 'play' and hey presto!" The machine selected only one of the four discs and dropped it onto the turntable with a barely audible thud.

Hot-diggity! Dog-ziggity! Boom! What you do to me... Perry Como louder than life, right there in Foss's front room. I had never imagined the like. I couldn't believe it. Our gramophone was the wind-up type, tall and tinny.

"Whatever next!" I said.

"This..." said Foss, flipping a switch and changing the wondrous machine to radio mode.

This is the BBC Home Service. Here is the nine o'clock news read by Alvoir Liddell.

Clear and loud, no static, no fading, none of the outer space oscillations that came from Dad's Bakelite wireless. Those few moments in front of razor-edge technology etched grooves in my mind every bit as deep as those in the records. From that moment on I measured and marked time in music.

"I know just where it's going," said Foss. "It looks like a sideboard and it's going against the window wall at the new house when we move next week."

Pigging Nora! Moving house! It had slipped my mind totally.

"Sorry, Mr. Stanley. We're moving today and they'll be waiting for me. Bye!"

"But I've got Frank Ifield's new 'un."

"Sorry. Mus' rush. Tarah!" And I plodged through the mud and puddles around the top of the houses and into the street just in time to see the moving van trundle around the corner and out of sight at the opposite end of the village.

"Oi! I'm still here, I'm not with Mam! I'm still here, come back! Oi!" A fresh sheet of rain swept up King Street and covered the silvery tyre tracks left by the truck. When it became apparent that the driver and my dad weren't going to turn around, I sat down on the front step—the door was locked—and pondered my dilemma. The step was wet and muddy from foot traffic, but as it was at the leeward side of the house most of the rain splashed onto the forlorn grey flagstones between me and the engorged gutter. Occasional raindrops, fat and cold, dripped from the eaves and smashed on my head like sparrow's eggs. By the time the water trickled through my hair and down my face it was warm and maddeningly itchy. My shoes were saturated and when I curled my feet I could feel the waterlogged socks wet against my frozen toes.

"Wish I had a hat."

Beaker's mother always made him wear a hat. Mostly a schoolboy cap like posh kids wore. I thought about sheltering in their old house – the doors had been stolen and access was easy. But the lead flashing from the roof was also gone, and previous downpours had soaked the plaster so the house smelled like a cross between wet cardboard and dry mice. Mam had warned us not to play in there as the joists had gone the same way as the floorboards and the house was a shell.

"A sea shell?" I asked.

"No, son. More like a bombshell, only without the bang."

Monty McBain's cat, left behind when they moved, came from nowhere and sat on the step beside me. Monty's dad had told him it had died and gone to live with Jesus, which turned out to be true, almost. It took up residence underneath the Methodist chapel where it seemed quite content. Unfortunately, the 'Little Darlin' came by three days later and mashed flat the house of God.

I'd never seen a wet cat before. This one looked like an animated oil rag and stank to the heights.

"Hello, Corky," A big drip smacked him on the head and he closed one eye in resigned disgust. "They forgot me. But they'll be back any second. My dad thinks I went earlier with my mam, but I never." Clouds pushed closer together and the light faded a bit.

"All the kids'll be in class now. I bet it's nearly milk time. I'm s'pose to be milk-monitor this week. Wonder who'll do that," The cat shook his head and shivered. "They'll be back any second. You could live in our back yard now. Dad won't chuck stones any more. We've shifted." I wiped my nose along my sleeve. "Wish I had a hat."

Something broke the skyline at the top of the hill to my left. It was Spike Batty. Spike was always by himself since his dad had gone to prison. None of the other kids was allowed to play with him and had soon got into a habit of interrupting our games and punching someone. Danny Bligh and my brothers had kept me safe before, but now there was only me and a calico cat.

Two seconds after I made this observation there was only me. Corky took off with the start that only cats display—like they suddenly remember an urgent appointment in another place. Obviously he had met Spike before.

"Shiftin', eh?"

"Yeah."

"Where's everybody at?"

"They left without me. They'll be back any second."

Spike leaned back to look up at the house. He pushed a finger up his nose further than I thought it possible for one to go. Without looking at it, he slipped it into his mouth and continued to peruse the building.

"Plenty floorboards an' stuff," he murmured.

"What do you mean?" I challenged.

"Nowt. Just saying, like. Plenty floorboards and stuff."

"You better not go in. I'll get the bobby to yer."

"You'll what?"

I knew I'd said the wrong thing, but a fire had suddenly built up inside that drove me to protect that house from the attention of the likes of Spike Batty. For some reason I was filled with hatred and I felt like bashing him. Of course, he was two years older than me, and twice the size. Taking a swing would be like committing suicide. Have you ever noticed that when an impossible compulsion takes control of you, time seems to pass at about one tenth the normal rate? My clenched fist wormed a curious path through the air toward

Spike's nose. He was saying something, but the words were slow and at least an octave below what human ears could easily detect. When I made contact, there was a sickening dull thud, not at all like the crack that rent the air when John Wayne belted someone. Spike's head moved backward not more that a few inches. He didn't even blink. Then time caught up, and I heard him say quite clearly.

"You bugger." Spike would never make a good boxer. His moves were telegraphed to the extent that I was able to avoid the punch by ducking under it. He hit the door and really surprised himself. I took off into the rain and legged it down King Street with Spike just a few paces behind. I made a plan... turn right at the bottom of the street and run back up Albion Street and then up to Black Road and... Gotcha! ... I ran straight into Nutty Wicker.

"Watch it, Mr. Wicker! Spike Batty's after me."

"Well, he's gone now, son. What ever has happened?" He took an enormous handkerchief out from somewhere under his de-mob coat and wiped the water from my face. He was wearing a bright yellow sou'wester and the biggest pair of Wellington boots I ever saw.

"I got left behind when the van left," I had caught my breath and felt secure now that Nutty had shown up. He pulled a worn umbrella from inside the voluminous coat and spread it over the two of us.

"How on earth did you manage that?" he said. "Never mind, they'll be back for you any second. Pigging Nora, you're a sight! Here, have a Fisherman's Friend." And he gave me a tiny tablet that put fire in my belly. We walked back up the street to the house and he sat on the step beside me, right where the cat had been. He produced a wax-paper package from some other compartment of the magic coat and offered me a huge cheese sandwich. Just the kind I liked, with Hoe's chutney.

"You know, sometimes we've got to get on with things. All things must pass. You'll forgive this," and he nodded at the house. "You'll live in the new town and find new friends, and before long you'll only have the fond memories. But remember this village has no hot water, most of the biffies are outside, and you can get bashed for next to nowt. There's new times coming for you, Philip. Sometimes it's as well to scrape off your shoe and move on."

Finally, as I polished off the last of the sandwich, the van came back into the street with a bang of blue smoke. The lights flashed on and off and I stood up.

"I'll come back and visit you, Mr. Wicker."

"You'll always find a welcome, whether you come or not. She likes you," he said, tapping the side of his nose. "And when she likes someone, she never lets go. Here's yer dad."

The van door swung open and down stepped my dad, shaking his head slowly and tut-tutting,

"Get in. Half way there we were. Get in you soft egg."

Nutty gave me a leg up.

"Here," he said. "Something for yer pocket." He stuffed a bag of hazelnuts under my pullover and slammed the door shut. As the driver ground the gears into place, I looked through the window to wave goodbye. Nutty wore a face-filling grin, and spreading his arms wide, began to dance along the drenched flagstones.

"We'll meet again, don't know where, don't know when, but I know we'll meet again some sunny day..."

I bounced up and down on the leatherette seat as the van negotiated the potholes in the road. Dad put his arm across my shoulder and pushed my matted hair back from my face. He heaved a heavy sigh.

"Fourteen years I lived in that house," he said. Then he looked at me and smiled softly. "Can't for the life of me remember breaking *two* mirrors."

~ • ~

28840392R00075

Made in the USA
Charleston, SC
23 April 2014